ZACH

TOREY HOPE: THE LATER YEARS

A.D. ELLIS

A.D. Ellis

Zach

Torey Hope:
The Later Years

A.D. Ellis
www.facebook.com/adellisauthor

Cover Updated 2019
A.D. Ellis

QUOTES OF INSPIRATION

*I hate waiting. But if waiting means being able to be with you.
I will wait for as long as forever to be with you, my best friend.
--Unknown*

*You are my best friend, my shoulder to lean on, the one person I
know I can count on, you're the love of my life, you're my one
and only, you're my everything. --Unknown*

*The best type of relationship is one where you're not only in
love, but you're each other's best friend. --Unknown*

To all those people lucky enough to fall in love with their best friend.

INTRODUCTION

If you're already a reader of the Torey Hope stories, I hope you're as happy with Zach and Zoey's story as I am. While I love all the Torey Hope characters, Zach was one of those who blended into the background pretty easily when I was writing the other stories. Great guy, but he got overshadowed a lot.

I absolutely fell in love with Zach in this story. I really got to know him, and watching him love Zoey just warmed my heart.

If you're not already a reader of Torey Hope, I hope Zach's story will touch you in some way. And, I invite you to read the other books in these series. Come visit Torey Hope, you'll never want to leave.

A NOTE FROM THE AUTHOR

For those who like a little narrative along with a family tree. Here are the families of Torey Hope. Meet the Morgans, the Jordans, the Deckers, and the Martins. If the family tree image is hard for you to see on your device, you can click here to find it on my website.

John and Cindy Morgan have twin boys Nate and Nicky Morgan.

Nicky Morgan married Carly Malone and had children Zachary Malone Morgan and Alyson Elizabeth Morgan.

Nate Morgan married Libby Decker and had children Abigail Emerson Morgan and twins Decker Nathaniel and Sawyer Nicholas Morgan.

Libby Decker is sister to **Audrey Decker**, both are

daughters of **Captain Robert Decker** and the late **Lois Decker**. Robert later married **Janie**.

Audrey Decker married **Jeremiah Jordan**. Jeremiah had a son, **Beckett**, from a previous marriage. Jeremiah and Audrey had **Megan Elise Jordan** and **Kendrick Robert Jordan**. Beckett got married in the first book of this series to a girl named Kenja.

Jeremiah is the son of **Jack and Judy Jordan**.

Captain Robert Decker had an estranged brother, Richard who was married to Corrine and they had a daughter named **Josie**. Josie married Jeremiah Jordan's best friend, **Kyle Martin** and they had children **Zoey Belle Martin** and **Asher Jeremiah Jordan**.

REGARDING THE CENTER+

This is a local community center in Torey Hope. In the first series, Nicky Morgan (Zach's dad) attended what was then known as The Center. This place runs educational programs, especially for students struggling in public schools, along with various programs revolving around the arts, sports, and fitness. When Zach, Decker, Sawyer, and Kendrick returned to Torey Hope from college, they took over the business, which many members of the family are involved with in some way, and renamed it The Center+.

Decker is the manager, his girlfriend, Katie, is the assistant manager. Sawyer is in charge of the art programs, including painting, pottery, dance, etc. He also works closely with his boyfriend, Luke, in the martial arts programs. Kendrick is in charge of the sports programs. Zach is the advertising executive. Many of the parents are also involved with programs at The Center+.

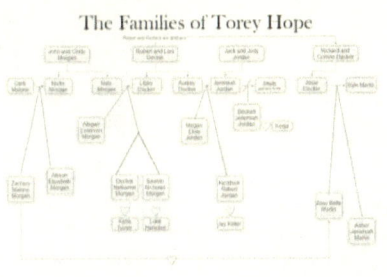

The Families of Torey Hope

Real-life Contemporary Romance by A.D. Ellis

1
_____

"Zach, would you like to meet the new baby?" His mom, Carly Morgan, asked warmly from her comfy position on the couch.

At five, and with his own baby sister only a few months old, he really had no interest in this new baby. But Aunt Josie was proud of her new arrival, so he shuffled his feet over to glance down at the baby his mother was holding.

Something in his stomach did flip-flops when the precious baby girl's eyes locked with his. Reaching a small hand out to touch her downy head, he sighed deeply, "She's so pretty."

He loved his baby sister, Aly. But the immediate connection he felt to his cousin, Zoey, rushed through his young body and mind at a speed which was too much to comprehend.

Letting the tiny bundle on his mom's lap grip his finger, he smiled and cooed at her in a way he'd never live down if his cousins ever found out about it.

"I think she likes you, Zach." The baby's mother, Josie Martin, spoke softly. "She's got a tight grip, huh?"

He'd let his baby sister hold his finger in much the same way, but it hadn't melted his heart the way it did then. Of course he loved the new baby at his own house, she was his sister so he sort of had to love her.

But, this baby wasn't his sister. He didn't have to live with her or love her. But he immediately did, love her that is. His brain couldn't quite grasp the feeling he was having, but he knew he would love her for the rest of his life.

"Hey there, Zoey Belle, I'm Zach. I promise to be your best friend and take care of you forever." He brushed his lips across her forehead, "I love you, pretty baby."

"Mom! Aly won't stop messing with me, please tell her to stop." Zach's ten-year-old voice traveled up the stairs from his parent's basement apartment in his grandparents' home.

Carly smiled at Josie as she headed to the stairway door just off the kitchen. Josie had brought her five-year-old daughter, Zoey, over to play with Aly. Zoey and Zach were playing wonderfully together, but Aly seemed to be cramping their style.

"Aly, sweetie, come up here for a bit and have a snack." Carly's soft voice lured her daughter up the steps.

"I wasn't bothering him, Mommy. I just wanted to play with Zoey, but she wanted to color with Zach. They always think they have to do everything together." Aly pouted as she sat down to eat some apple slices and milk.

"Zoey isn't used to having a big brother around, sweetie. When we come over here to visit she thinks having Zach to play with is pretty special." Josie tried to console the little girl.

"You and Zoey get to see each other in class every single day, you're best friends. She doesn't get to spend as much time with Zach. Finish your snack and maybe the three of you can watch a movie." Carly smoothed her daughter's hair and smiled at Josie over the top of her head.

The women had talked at length between themselves and their sisters-in-law, Libby Morgan and Audrey Jordan. Zach had developed a loving and protective streak ten miles wide the instant he'd laid eyes on Zoey as a baby. He had little patience for his own sister, but he would play any and every game Zoey asked him to. He helped her learn to walk, tie her shoes, and ride a bike without a second thought. When the families were together it could be counted on that Zach and Zoey would be joined at the hip.

Using a reference to a popular book series turned film

phenomenon, the families had always joked that Zach had imprinted on Zoey the very first time he'd met her.

"It's a good thing that's all made-for-fiction stuff since they're cousins." Judy Morgan, one of three grandmas in the clan smiled.

"Technically, they aren't. And who says cousins can't be soul mates?" Audrey watched Zach hold Zoey's hand as he helped her cross a damp, mossy log in the backyard.

"Luckily we aren't dealing with vampires and shape shifters. Just two precious kids who love each other very much." Grandma Janie laughed in reference to the fictional characters who *imprinted* in the books and movies.

"Well, I for one am happy to know Zach will be Zoey's friend and protect her. All little girls need a brother, or daddy, or cousin, or friend to do that for them. I'm glad to know all my granddaughters have that." Jack Jordan spoke up.

Coming back to the present, Carly and Josie watched as Aly slid from her chair and took a deep breath as if fortifying herself to put up with her brother and best friend.

After a few more cups of coffee and a couple hours of visiting, Josie gathered up her sleeping infant, Asher, and the mothers headed downstairs to check on the three older children.

"That is absolutely adorable. Take a picture, be sure to send it to me." Josie smiled at the three kids, lumped together on the sofa while the movie credits ran.

Zach was nestled in the corner of the couch with Zoey snuggled under his arm. She held Aly close to her other side.

Zach was as rough-and-tumble as his three male cousins, but he never complained about spending time with Zoey. Having Aly tag along wasn't top on his priority list, but having his sister with them was the price he paid for spending time with his favorite girl.

"Zoey Belle, don't move."

His voice was serious.

She was only five, but Zoey must have immediately recognized the fear in his voice because she stopped dead in her tracks.

He walked up slowly behind her. Grabbing her shoulders he quickly whispered in her ear, "You just stepped on the edge of a yellow jacket nest, pretty girl. I'm going to spin you around, and I want you to run before they get really angry, okay?"

He breathed a sigh of relief that she didn't cry or make any other loud noises. She hadn't disturbed the nest much, but one more step would have likely caused the stinging insects to start swarming.

"Once I spin you around, run and get the Captain, okay?"

When she nodded, Zach continued, "Okay, one, two, three, *run!*" He spun her around and pushed her slightly.

Knowing the yellow jackets would sting that which was closest, he stood his ground at the edge of the nest, watching the little girl run to their grandfather.

His heart caught in his throat when she stumbled just a few feet away. Her worried face looked back at him desperately, her fear of him getting hurt was evident.

"I'm fine, Zoey. Just run!"

The movement and noise at the edge of the nest had been enough to stir the jacks up, and he heard the ferocious buzzing building around his feet, working its way up to his head.

Once he knew she was far enough away, Zach took five giant steps away from the nest, batting at the angry buzzing around his head. He knew he'd been stung at least a couple times, the hot, burning stings were making themselves known quickly.

Ever grateful for the well-prepared Captain, Zach rushed to Zoey as his grandfather stalked toward the nest with a fire extinguisher. Zach held Zoey close to his side as the Captain sprayed the nest and surrounding area with the foam.

"That will keep them cold and slow them down for a bit. It's always wise to bring a fire extinguisher on a trip to the woods, you never know what it may be useful for." The Captain winked at the children, and then ushered them away from the paralyzed colony.

Once they'd reached their camp, Zach's mom and aunts had gotten word of the incident and had a paste of baking soda ready to rub on his wounds.

"You got stung!" Zoey's bottom lip quivered as she watched her aunt spread the soothing paste on several angry red stings.

"I'm sorry, Zach. I didn't know the nest was there. I didn't want you to get hurt, I was just wanting to climb that tree." Tears poured down the girl's face.

"Zoey Belle, no harm, no foul. You didn't get me stung on purpose. I'd rather it was me getting stung than you. Once my stings are all covered we'll go find the best climbing tree in the whole woods. Whatdya say? Ready to climb trees with me, pretty girl?" He winked at her, and tried to concentrate on climbing trees rather than on the throbbing stings.

"So, if you *had* to pick a girl to kiss, who would it be?" Kendrick, the cousin who had started to show the most interest in girls at their tender age of 11, wagged his eyebrows and challenged the other three to name a girl.

"I don't want to kiss any girl. The girls in our class are always giggling and saying stupid stuff. I don't get them at all." Decker, the most level-headed of the crew, shook his head in disgust. He had yet to meet any girl who seemed worth the bother.

"I don't know, man. Maybe Katie Smith? If I *had* to, not because I want to kiss any girl." Sawyer's answer followed his twin's, and made his face blush.

"I don't even like girls." Zach had rolled his eyes.

"Oh, right, you just have Zoey at your side every second of the day if possible." Kendrick shot back.

"Not because I want to *kiss* her. She's my friend." Zach defended.

"But, let's say when we're older, and she's not just a little girl, would you want to kiss her then?" Kendrick challenged.

"I don't know, I don't even want to talk about kissing girls. And, she will always be younger than me. Plus, isn't it like illegal to kiss your cousin or something?" Zach felt a bit strange to be having the conversation.

"If you think about it, she's not *truly* your cousin. We all call them Aunt Josie and Uncle Kyle, but they aren't related to Uncle Nicky or Aunt Carly at all. Sawyer and Kendrick and I are distantly related to them, but Aly and Zach aren't at all." Decker presented the facts.

"So, would you want to kiss her when we're older?" Kendrick wouldn't let it die.

"Sure, yeah, fine. I'd kiss her if we were older. But only if I *had* to." Exasperated, Zach walked away from the ridiculous hypothetical talk. He loved Zoey. Their friendship wasn't the same as his with his male cousins, but she was one of his closest friends. He didn't want to think about ruining things by kissing her.

2

"*Z*ach, I just want to go home. I hate it here without Aly." She leaned into his long, lean torso and let his tanned, lanky arms wrap around her.

At age 14, Zach was loving his position as Jr. Camp Counselor at Torey Hope Summer Camp, but his favorite girl was miserable. She and Aly had made grand plans for their first summer camp experience, but his sister had come down with strep throat the day before shipping out.

Knowing all of her older cousins, including the older girls Megan and Abby, were either counselors or junior counselors, Zoey's parents had encouraged her to try camp on her own. She had several friends from school with her at the camp, but missing home and her best friend brought Zoey to a low point.

"Shhh, it's okay, pretty girl. You've got almost every

cousin in the family here at the camp to take care of you. You've already made it three days, I know you can make it three more." He hugged her close and kissed her head.

Zach thought camp was about the best thing he'd done in his short life. He got to spend the day with his cousins, play sports, swim, eat in the cafeteria, and watch his pretty co-counselors. At age 9, Zoey wasn't filling out a swimsuit in any way that would make him or any boy take notice, although he was determined to make her comfortable and get her through her first camp experience. But, the giggling he heard behind him quickly reminded him that he'd let Kendrick set him up for some secret kisses in the woods.

Pulling Zoey closer, he rubbed her arms as he spoke. "Listen, Zo, you've got craft time. Then you promised to help the leaders with weeding the garden. After that I'll see you in the cafeteria. I promise I'll do my best to sneak out for a little bit tonight so I can see you before lights out. Is it a deal?"

He knew he could get in trouble for sneaking out, and especially for going to the girls' side of camp after dark, but he figured he could explain his indiscretions away by pointing out he was just checking on his young cousin.

Several hours later, his mind was still on the kisses he had shared with Courtney, one of his fellow junior counselors. He remembered a conversation he'd had with his cousins a few years earlier about kissing, and he recalled not being too keen on the idea.

But, after a bit of messing around in the woods with a girl

his age, he felt like he could possibly reconsider. He had enjoyed the scent of her coconut oiled skin and sunbathed hair; the warmth of her skin as his hands ran down her arms had sent strange feelings rushing through his body. He shivered a bit as he recalled the friction between his bare chest and her bikini-top-clad breasts. Keeping his hands on her waist until she brazenly moved them to her chest, he slowly brought his lips down on hers.

He had been on sensation overload and still felt like his body was short-circuiting. But, as he walked through the woods with a surprise for his favorite girl, he tried to wrap his head around the chaos and confusion of his feelings. He enjoyed the physical contact with Courtney; he had a feeling most guys his age would enjoy having a pretty girl to kiss and caress. But his heart felt guilty about what he'd done. He knew he couldn't kiss and rub on Zoey in that way, and he didn't even let that enter his mind because it made him slightly ill. As his heart and body warred against their contrasting feelings, Zach realized that his heart, body, and mind would likely struggle with the conflicting feelings for many years to come.

He loved Zoey. Period.

He liked looking at other girls, girls his age. He really liked kissing them.

But, when it all came right down to it, if made to choose, he'd pick Zoey hands-down every single time. He knew things were weird with their age difference, but he felt strongly in his heart that he'd wait and fight for his girl for as long as it took.

Coming up to the girls' side of camp, he smiled as he crept to her cabin. He'd snuck a piece of chocolate cake from the birthday party they'd been having for one of the senior counselors. Wrapped in wax paper, packed with a fork and an icy milk courtesy of the cafeteria, the cake was cradled in Zach's arms like precious cargo.

At the shadowy edge of her cabin, Zach crouched under her window. He knew she slept next to the window, but he wasn't sure if she was already in bed. They had about forty-five minutes before lights out. Popping his head up slowly, he peeked in the brightly glowing window, holding his breath in fear of getting caught.

He smiled when he saw her sitting on her bottom bunk. Tapping on the window lightly, he put a finger to his lips to encourage her to be quiet. With a slight nod of his head, he gestured toward the door, indicating she should join him outside.

A few moments later, he heard leaves rustling. They met up in the small grove of trees on the dark side of her cabin.

"You came! I didn't think you would." The surprise and joy was evident in her voice.

"Hey, pretty girl, I will always, *always* come for you. I just had a couple things to get done before I could sneak over." He produced the cake dramatically.

"Yummy! I didn't really like dinner tonight, so that cake

looks delicious." She grabbed the fork and stabbed a large bite of the cake.

"Did you get some already?" She asked around her mouthful of chocolatey goodness.

"I had a small piece over on the boys' side. I sort of thought you'd share with me." The joking laughter in his voice couldn't be hidden.

Smiling up at him, she swallowed the cake. "Oh, sorry. Sure, you can have a couple *small* bites of mine."

She held a tiny bite of cake out in front of him, teasing as she swirled it around in front of his mouth.

He grabbed her wrist, holding the meandering cake still and captured the bite. They played airplane back and forth until the cake was gone, then shared the cold milk.

Gathering the evidence of their late-night snack, Zach threw it all away in the nearby trashcan.

"So, were you kissing Courtney?"

The question was blunt and took him off-guard.

"Why do you ask?"

Hoping to buy some time, he swirled possible answers through his mind.

"Well, I heard the counselors talking, and Courtney said, 'I kissed Zach,' so I figured she was talking about you. But then I thought about how you and the guys say kissing makes you want to puke, so I couldn't decide if it was you or not."

He leaned himself back against a tree and gathered her to him.

"Kissing is sort of weird, Zoey. I've tried it, and it's not as gross as I once thought it might be. But, I don't know that I'm ready to go around kissing everything with lips." He chuckled and ran a hand absently through her hair when she laughed at his answer.

"Well, kissing *is* gross and I will never kiss a boy or ask him to kiss me. Yuck."

As he stood to head back to his side of the camp, Zach fought the rival feelings of being relieved Zoey wasn't planning on kissing any boys, and feeling frustrated about the fact that *one day* he wanted her to want to kiss him.

"Can you move that rock over there?" Zoey pointed toward the edge of the newly dug garden plot.

Zach wiped the sweat from his eyes as he bent to heft the rock. After moving it at least seven other times, he was convinced it should have been referred to as a boulder, but he adjusted his grip and heaved the rock to its next new location.

At 15, he was sure there was *something* he could be doing which would be better than designing, digging, planting, and decorating a garden over the weekend. But then he looked at her face. Her bright eyes, her rosy cheeks, the determined look of contemplation, all of those things caused his heart to swell, and he knew there was nowhere he'd rather spend his weekend than in the garden they built together.

"Nah, man, my stomach can't handle another round on that thing." Zach's past rollercoaster riding partner in crime, Kendrick, looked a little green around the gills.

"Come on! The line is short, later today it will be longer. Someone needs to ride with me so I don't have to stand in line by myself like a loser." Zach looked around at his cousins.

Kendrick was obviously going to need a breather before he got back in line. Decker shook his head and gestured toward his twin, Sawyer.

"Sorry, I promised Sawyer we'd go watch the Chinese acrobats. They are only here today and only have one performance left."

Looking at his nearby surroundings at the theme park they visited each summer, Zach scanned the crowd in hopes someone in his family was in the vicinity and willing to ride.

When his eyes landed on Zoey, he had a sudden inspiration. Last year she'd still been a fraction of an inch too short for the big rollercoasters. But he was sure she had grown enough since then. He just needed to convince her it wasn't as bad as Kendrick was letting on.

Riding his adrenaline high from the last go-round on the monstrous coaster, Zach snuck up behind Zoey and Aly while they were trying on sunglasses at one of the numerous souvenir stores.

"Gotcha!"

He laughed when she squealed. His heart grew warm to feel her relax in his arms as soon as she realized it was him.

"Zach! You scared me to death! Put me down!" She giggled in her sweet 11 year old way, and punched him in the arm.

"Ouch, watch it, Zo! You could hurt a guy." He ruffled her hair. "On second thought, keep practicing that right hook and your uppercut; you'll need to put the boys in their place this coming year at school."

He knew it was crazy, but he wasn't looking forward to her starting sixth grade. She had always been pretty, but she seemed to be doing what grownups referred to as *coming into herself*, and Zach didn't want to even think about the middle school punks who would be flirting with her.

"So, pretty girl, did you realize that you're finally tall enough to ride the big roller coasters with me?" He asked while wagging his eyebrows.

"Ugh, don't remind me! I really don't think those coasters are for me, Zach. I like the tamer ones that I've been riding for a few years. I'm not the same thrill-seeker as you and Kendrick are." She wrinkled her nose, and stared up at the towering coaster in question.

"Please, Zoey Belle?" He knew he was pleading, but he wanted to ride again, and he had a feeling if he ever got her *on* a big coaster he'd have trouble ever getting her *off*. He just had a hunch that she would be as much of an adrenaline junky as himself.

"Fine!" She placed the sunglasses back on the rack and rolled her eyes at Aly.

"I'll ride the darn roller coaster with you *one* time! But that's it! After that, you'll have to find some other poor sucker to ride with you."

She grabbed him by the arm and began marching him toward the line.

Looking dramatically over her shoulder she shouted to Aly, "If I die on this ride, you can have all my clothes and shoes!"

They both laughed at Aly when she pumped her fist and yelled, "Yes!"

The wait for their turn passed quickly because they joked and talked the whole time. It amazed him how his sister at age 11 was annoying, obnoxious, and a general pain, but Zoey at the same age was a breath of fresh air, someone he didn't mind standing in line with, a genuinely fun person to be around.

As they climbed into their seats and pulled the heavy harness contraptions over their heads and shoulders, he could feel Zoey's trepidation.

"Hey, pretty girl, no worries. I'm right here." He reached over and held her hand.

Her face brightened with relief. Squeezing his hand she smiled over at him, "Thanks, Zach. I'm glad my first time is with you."

Two minutes thirty seconds later they pulled back into

the loading dock, and Zach knew he had her hooked. Climbing from the car, he barely kept himself upright when she threw herself at him and begged to ride again.

"I don't know, Zo. I promised I'd let you ride one time and then find some other poor sucker to ride with me. I better go see if Kendrick is ready." He tried to hide a smile as he spoke.

"No! I mean, he looked pretty sick. I'll ride with you since he's not feeling well." Her attempt to stop herself from blushing was futile.

"There's no one I'd rather be scared out of my mind with than you." She squeezed his hand as they waited in line for the next big thrill ride of that summer.

"I'll always be with you, through good time, bad times, and scary times." He ruffled her hair and pulled her into a hug.

At age 16 he meant every word he said, and she believed him wholeheartedly.

"Мом! Will you please tell Zach that he HAS to drive us to the mall?" Aly's exasperated plea was like finger nails on a chalkboard.

"No, Aly, I will not tell Zach he HAS to drive you and Zoey to the mall." Carly Morgan smoothed her daughter's hair and smiled softly.

Turning to her son she continued, "But, I *will* tell him

that his dad and I both have to be at work today so we can't take you girls to get the items you need for tonight's dance. And I'll tell him that lunch and gas money will be provided should he decide to be a great guy and taxi you girls around for a couple hours."

Zach groaned.

"No fair, Mom."

He laughed good-naturedly and spoke to Aly.

"Fine, tell Zoey we'll be there in ten minutes. But I get to choose where we eat lunch. And we're *only* there for the items you need, this isn't going to be an all day excursion."

He shook his head and rolled his eyes as his sister whooped on her way to call Zoey.

"Thank you, Zach. The mall is just too far away for them to get there themselves, not that I'd feel all that comfortable with that anyway, and your dad and I both need to be at The Center today." She patted his cheek and handed him money for gas and food.

"You really are a great big brother and cousin."

Three hours later he was feeling anything but great. He had survived lunch. He had survived sitting in front of stores while the girls shopped. He'd even survived holding their many shopping bags from time to time.

The part that was about to kill him was the recap of purchases complete with a show-and-tell of each item.

Bras and thongs. They were 12 for God's sake. Did they really need bras and thongs for the fall dance at school?

"Yes, dear brother, we *do* need these things for the dance. Every girl loves a pretty new bra, and most girls wear thong underwear all the time. Besides, even if we didn't mostly wear thongs, our dresses both require them so we don't have panty lines." Aly rolled her eyes and shook her head, exasperated at Zach's questioning of their purchases.

"For the love of all that's holy, you two better be making sure those bras and thongs stay nice and hidden under your dresses so no punk-ass middle school kid has to get a foot up his ass."

The girls just giggled and continued to look through their undergarment, shoe, and jewelry purchases.

From his spot in the driver's seat, Zach fumed and wondered if his parents and Zoey's knew what their girls were wearing under their clothing.

"He's not coming." Zoey's dejected voice hitched as she attempted to swallow her tears.

"What do you mean he's not coming? Is he just meeting us there?" Aly questioned as she held the arm of her date to the evening's dance at school.

"No, I mean he's not coming. At all." Tears flooded her eyes.

Zach gathered her in his arms and let her cry against his chest.

"Aly, Justin's mom is waiting to drive you. You two go ahead to the dance. Zoey will be there in a bit." Zach shooed his sister and her date out the door.

"Zoey Belle, stop crying, that little asshole isn't worth your tears." His thumbs swiped gently at the tears running down her cheeks.

"I know he's not worth it, I was just looking forward to dancing and having fun. I honestly barely even liked him. I just wanted a date and I wanted to get dressed up for tonight. Now I have no date, no dancing, and no reason to be dressed up."

She buried her head in his chest, "Can you just take me home, please?"

"No can do, pretty girl." He steered her by her shoulders and walked her toward the bathroom.

"Why, do you have a date tonight?"

"Yes, I have a date. In fact, I need to go change. Fix your face and hair, although I think you look beautiful no matter what. I'll be ready in just a minute."

When Zach returned to the front room, Zoey began the trudge to his vehicle.

"Can you at least drop me off first so I don't feel like a date-crasher?" She wrinkled her nose and tried to laugh.

"We'll see." He tried to hide his smirk.

Pulling into the school lot, he realized that most of the cars were either chaperones or parents dropping students off.

Very few of the dates to tonight's dance were old enough to drive.

"Zach, I really don't want to come here, can you just take me home. Please?" Her eyes sparkling as she took in the busyness of the school and the flair of the dance belied her statement.

"Well, it seems my date wants to come to this school dance, so that's what I'm going to do." He jumped from the car, walking to her side and opening the door.

She took his hand and allowed herself to be pulled from the car. Questioning eyes fell on him.

"Let it be said, I have the prettiest date here tonight. Hands down."

He hugged her close when she wrapped her arms around his neck.

"Thank you, Zach. You're the best."

Avoiding the curious stares, Zach spent the evening talking to former teachers, dancing with Zoey and her big group of friends, and smiling when he saw how happy his girl was.

He may have also made sure a little visit was paid to a certain punk-ass kid before the night was over. He knew Kendrick would get the point across to the kid, leave no incriminating evidence, and never say a word. His cousin had changed a lot over the past year or so. Zach couldn't pinpoint what had happened, but it was hard to watch and even harder still to be clueless about it. But, he knew Kendrick would take care of the little shit who hurt Zoey. Kendrick had changed, but Zach still trusted him with his life.

"Thank you, Zach. Thanks for saving me. Tonight was great." She smiled at him across the car's interior. "The only thing missing was my first kiss. Don't worry, I let you stand in for my absentee date, I won't make things any more awkward by asking you to kiss me."

They both laughed. Her innocently, him somewhat awkwardly.

As he drove away, he wondered what a date between them could look like in about five years. Would he ever know?

3

"Kiss me, Zach. Please?" Her sparkling green eyes mesmerized him. He glanced at her full, pink mouth and knew he would give in to her request. He needed to tell her no, hold her off. It was wrong. But, the desire he felt for her was too strong. Just one kiss, then they'd have to talk. They needed to go back to just friends. He couldn't risk hurting her or losing her.

"Please, kiss me. I want you to be my first kiss, I don't want to share that with anyone else." She pleaded and gripped his shirt with her tiny fists.

With no more thoughts of right or wrong, he lowered his head. The scent of lemon sunshine overtook his senses and his body lit on fire when his lips touched hers.

He was too old for her, he should be kissing girls his own age. Five years would maybe be no big deal when they were twenty-five and thirty. But five years was a very big deal at the moment.

But her lips took over and he was helpless to stop.

"Zach..." Her voice sounded far away.

He moaned into her mouth.

"Zach..."

Pulling back slightly, he ran a thumb over her swollen bottom lip.

"Zach!"

He jumped as a fist connected with his shoulder.

Opening his eyes and glancing around he realized he had fallen asleep on Zoey's couch as they watched television.

"Were you dreaming? It looked like you were trying to kiss someone."

Zoey laughed and tickled him, "Ohhh, Zach wants to *kiss a girl*. Who is it? Tell me, I promise I won't tell Aly." Zoey continued to tease, but Zach had woken in a grumpy funk.

"Knock it off, Zoey Belle. I wasn't dreaming, and I don't want to kiss anyone. I need to get home and do my homework. I'll see you tomorrow. Okay?"

He headed home, glad he had homework to distract him. The guilty thoughts about his feelings toward Zoey danced in his head like tiny fairies, and they were all a-twitter about how messed up in the head he was to be thinking of his younger cousin that way.

Technically, she's not your cousin.

"Yeah, well, she most definitely *is* five years younger than me and there's *no way* to explain that one away." Zach shook his head in disgust.

As he walked, he attempted to make sense of his feelings. He was attracted to girls at his high school, girls his own age. He loved their curves, their smiles, the scent of shampoo from their hair. He'd kissed a few of them, and it was nice. But, he never felt the urge to spend time with them outside of school.

Zoey was still just a little girl, he truly had no physical attraction to her at all, but his dreams took him to a time and place where they were both older. In his dreams, he saw Zoey as the knock-out he knew she would be as she grew up. But, he also saw her as his soul mate, his true love, the only one he wanted to spend his time with.

But then he'd wake up and reality would slap him in the face. He couldn't pine after his little cousin. He couldn't expect her to put her life on hold while she waited to grow up enough to make his feelings for her acceptable. No, they'd continue being best friends, and whoever they dated over the years would just have to accept that.

He hadn't realized how hard it was going to be. He sat in Zoey's room, something he'd done basically every day since she was old enough to have a room of her own, and held her as she cried.

"Zach, it's just not fair. You're my best friend and you're leaving for four years!" Zoey's tears fell on his shirt, leaving a damp trail on his chest.

"Zoey Belle, I have to go. You've known we're leaving for at least 2 years now. I'll be home for holidays. You'll be so busy with school and friends, you won't even have time to think about me."

He felt torn by his words. He *wanted* her to be busy with school and friends, but he also felt an ache in his heart knowing she'd probably move on without him.

"Zach, I've never been away from you. In my entire thirteen years I've *maybe* not seen you a couple days here and there. I don't want to forget about you, I love you."

Zoey sniffed her nose and looked up at him with pleading eyes.

"I know, pretty girl. I'm going to miss you too."

Zach held her close and kissed the top of her head.

"You're going to think this is stupid, and I feel like a complete dork saying it, but I totally wish we were the same age." Zoey's tears had made her nose stuffy.

Zach thought she sounded adorable. He gave her a questioning look.

Blushing, Zoey went on, "I guess this past year I've started looking at you more like a guy rather than just my best friend. I feel like we were meant to be together, I just don't understand why there has to be five years between us."

She bowed her head, and let her forehead rest on his chest.

Her muffled words floated to his ears, and he felt them straight to his heart.

"I love you, Zach. Like my best friend, yes, but more than that. I know you think I'm just a little girl, but you mean more to me than anyone ever could."

His heart soared, but the flight was short-lived as it quickly came crashing to the ground. He couldn't control time, couldn't make their ages work, at least not right then. He had to go off to school and live his life, just like Zoey needed to live her life in Torey Hope.

"Listen to me, Zoey Belle. I love you. You're my favorite girl. No one aside from us would get it right now, our ages are too far apart, they'd have a fit and think terrible things about me being so much older than you. We're going to live our lives, but our hearts belong to each other. No matter what you go through, no matter what I go through, our hearts will always come back here to Torey Hope, to each other." Zach pulled her in for a warm hug.

"What does that mean, Zach?" Zoey's eyes held a glimmer of hope.

"It means I love you, and I'll wait for you."

"Right, you'll go to college and not date other girls?" Zoey snorted. "I know you've kissed girls at school."

"No, I'll date and you'll have boyfriends, too. Yes, I've

kissed other girls, but none have held my heart the way you do." Zach rested his chin on top of her head.

"What if one of those girls you date takes my place as the holder of your heart?" Zoey looked doubtful.

"Not gonna happen." Zach pulled back to look in her eyes.

"Not gonna happen for me either. None of the boys in my class will ever take your place in my heart, Zach. There's no way. They can't compete with our friendship and our history." Zoey spoke with certainty. "But, you've never kissed me the way you kiss those girls at school. How do you know I'm worth the wait?"

He watched uncertainty and doubt flicker in her eyes.

"Zoey Belle, I've known you were worth the wait since the very first moment I laid eyes on you. We just have to wait a little longer than most." Zach teased her a bit, but inside it was killing him to know she was scared and worried.

"You could kiss me now." Her voice was barely a whisper.

"I could. But I won't." Zach spoke with finality.

As much as he loved her, the timing was all wrong. He was leaving for college, she was starting junior high. His love for her surpassed physical desires; she was his forever girl.

"We just have to hold tight to the journey ahead of us. I'll write my story while you write your own, and one day our stories will meet up again. When the timing is better, when we know who we are, when what we share can be accepted rather than frowned upon, *then* we can be together. But, until then, you're forever my favorite girl."

Zach had kissed her head and left with promises to text, and video chat, and call.

The next day he and his cousins drove off towards the next four years of their life. His future was bright, his heart was excited, and he felt ready for the next step. Except, a piece of his heart lay broken at the feet of his sweet Zoey Belle and wept for what they would miss for the next four years.

4

"Zoey's phone, talk to me." A cocky sounding, very much *male* voice answered when Zach attempted to call Zoey for the fourth time that day. He'd tried before and after his 8:00 a.m. class, at lunch, and now on his way out of his last class of the day. Zoey had called the day before, and he felt bad that he'd not heard the phone ringing from the shower.

"Who is this? Why do you have Zoey's phone?" Zach demanded.

"Who's this? Why are you calling Zoey's phone? Dude, you sound like some old guy. What a perv, calling a cute teenage girl's phone."

The cocky little asshole on the other end of the phone had no way of knowing it, but he was damn lucky a great distance separated them or he would have been laid flat.

"This is her best friend, Zach. Can I talk to Zoey, please?" He attempted to remain calm, but he didn't like the little punk answering Zoey's phone.

"Hey, Zoey, some old guy named Zach is on the phone. Do you want to talk to him?" The voice was muffled, but Zach knew it was meant to piss him off even more.

After some rustling, he heard her sweet voice and all anger faded away.

"Zach! I'm so glad you called! How's school? Are the classes hard? Do you miss me?" Her words rambled out in a rush.

"Zoey Belle, it's so good to hear your voice." He closed his eyes as he spoke, savoring the calm that came over him when she spoke.

"So, is your junior year going just as well as last year did?"

Zach could hear her moving around, then her voice was muffled as she spoke to whoever was with her.

"Hey, I'm going to be talking to Zach. Go ahead and get started on the problems and we can go over them when I'm done."

"Okay, so tell me about your classes." The smiled he knew was on her face could be heard in her words.

After talking for about ten minutes about his classes and the activities she and Aly had been taking part in, Zoey abruptly changed the subject.

"Are you dating anyone?" She whispered.

"No."

He thought it best to keep the answer simple. Yes, he'd gone out with a few girls since the semester started. And, yes, he'd occasionally kept his door closed and locked when said girls accompanied him back to the place he shared with his cousins. But, did these girls make his heart happy like Zoey? No. So, the less she knew, the better. At least that's what he told himself. In reality it was probably more accurate to say he didn't want to hurt her feelings or make her doubt him.

"What about you? Are you dating? Who was the little shit who answered your phone? Gotta tell you, Zo, he sounds like an asshole."

Zoey's giggles rang through the line, and he couldn't help but smile.

"That's Jason, he's my lab partner."

"Is that all he is?"

"Yes, that's all. We work on labs. He's also in some of my other classes. He's asked me out a few times, but so far I've only spent time with him in a big group. Don't worry, he's not you." She whispered the words, and his heart soared.

"Let me talk to him."

"What? No, Zach, there's no reason for that." Zoey protested.

"Zoey Belle, put him on the phone." Zach spoke in a way that left no room for argument.

After some muffled voices and rustling, the cocky voice returned. "Jason here, what can I do ya for?"

Zach rolled his eyes and pictured what a douche the kid had to be.

"Hiya, Johnathan." Zach smirked at the intentional misuse of the kid's name.

"It's *Jason* and I'm busy, what do you need?" Irritated, the kid huffed.

"Listen, *Jason*, Zoey Belle is my very favorite girl. If you do a single thing to hurt her, I will have to drive all the way back to Torey Hope and kick your ass. So, let's make it easier on everyone involved. Stay away from Zoey. Do your lab work, but nothing else. No touches, no kisses, no dates. Got it?" Zach felt a tightness in his chest as he spoke.

He knew it was unfair to sabotage something between the two if Zoey really liked the guy, but there was no way she could like a little piece of shit as arrogant and cocky as this Jason came across on the phone.

"Well, Zach, it was good talking to you. I'll take your suggestions under consideration, but I've got to tell you, my gut is saying you're pretty much shit out of luck. I mean, *you're* there, so far away. *I'm* here, with her, every day." Jason spoke snidely.

"Come to think of it, I'm going to end the suspense and let you know now. I'm going to have to pass on your offer."

The asshole continued in a sly whisper, "There will be plenty of touches, kisses, and dates if I have my way. In fact, just watching that fine little ass from across the room, I'm pretty sure there will be plenty of touching as this study session goes on."

"You little fucker!" Zach saw red.

"Zach, what's wrong?" Zoey was back on the line and oblivious to what the two had just talked about.

"Nothing, Zoey Belle." Taking a deep breath he attempted to calm himself. "Listen, Zo, I really don't like that kid. He's rude and cocky. Do your lab work alone or with someone else. Please? For me?"

Zach felt like a complete idiot asking, but he had a bad feeling about Jason.

Talking in a soft whisper, Zoey smiled through the phone. "Yeah, okay, Zach. We've got a couple more weeks of this lab and then we'll be assigned new partners. I'll be sure to switch then, okay?"

"Okay. Listen, I don't want to sound like a complete jerk, but I don't trust that guy. Don't be alone with him if you can keep from it." Zach's worry was evident.

"Hey, what did you call me about yesterday?" Attempting to change the subject to something less annoying, Zach inquired even though he was pretty sure he already knew what was coming.

"Oh! I almost forgot! I called to tell you that I'm getting my license this weekend!! Next time you come home I can drive you around town." She giggled as she spoke.

"That's great, Zo. I'm proud of you." Zach glanced at his watch and realized he needed to meet up with his cousins.

"Listen, pretty girl, I've got to head out. I'll talk to you tonight or tomorrow, okay? Text me anytime."

"Okay. Thanks for calling." Her disappointment was clear. "I love you, Zach."

"And I love you. Still my forever girl, right?" He tried to be jovial, but knowing she was sad broke his heart. Two more years. Just two more years then they could spend more time together. Of course, then they'd have the issue of Zoey going off to college, and the separation would begin all over again.

"Of course I'm still your forever girl." The tears made her voice catch before she disconnected the call.

As Zach walked to meet the guys for dinner he made a call to his Uncle Kyle. He wanted to be sure *Jason* wasn't spending too much time with his girl. Kyle needed to know the kid was a complete douche.

"I can't believe you guys came home!" Zoey ran out to the truck with huge hugs for her cousins and Zach. "You guys are so sweet, Grandma Cindy and Grandpa John will be so touched that you came home to celebrate their anniversary. Everyone is going to be so surprised! Thanks for trusting me to keep it a secret."

"You guys head on in, I'm going to steal Zoey for a few minutes." Zach nodded at the other guys.

"Sure thing, more food for me. You know there's always

something good to eat, even when they don't know we're coming." Kendrick rubbed his stomach dramatically. "And, Zach, if it only takes a minute, you're doing it wrong." He winked before bounding up the stairs in search of food.

Sawyer and Decker just shook their heads and followed him inside.

"Where are you stealing me away to?" Zoey giggled.

It felt so good to be back home, even if just for a couple days, and have her by his side.

"Well, I hate that I missed your birthday, and I thought I'd drag you away to give you your present." He'd been thinking of this moment the entire drive home. Was it too soon? Was it wrong? No, he wasn't planning anything outrageous, he just couldn't stand to wait any longer.

When they reached the garage, Zach ushered her inside. Not the most romantic place, but he knew the dinner would be starting soon, and he didn't want people to come searching.

"So, Zo, I've been thinking it over. There's still too much of an age difference for anything serious, but I can't stand the thought of you having your first kiss with anyone else. I'm actually surprised it's not happened yet." He stood behind her, content to hold her in his arms and talk quietly in her ear.

"I guess I've had a couple opportunities, but I think I've been holding out hoping my first kiss would be you. I mean, you've been there through most of my milestones, so it felt right that you be there for that too." She turned, wrapping her arms around his neck. "So, what's my belated birthday present?" Her voice held the hint of a hidden smile.

"Since I was there for all the firsts like first steps, writing your name, tying your shoes, and riding a bike, I agree that it's only appropriate that I be here for this momentous occasion." He winked at her, and tipped her chin up.

He was obviously a total glutton for punishment. Kissing her lightly on the lips, and pulling away without taking it any further took everything in him. How could a single brush of lips punch him in the gut so forcefully? This little impromptu birthday gift had just reminded him of how long they had until he could kiss her the way he really wanted, but it also cemented the fact that she was the only girl he'd ever truly long for, ever truly love.

"Happy belated birthday, pretty girl." He landed one last tiny peck on her mouth.

With her eyes still closed, she smiled, "Best birthday gift. Ever. Thank you."

The rest of the weekend went by in a blur of family togetherness. All too soon it was time for the guys to make the long trek back to school.

Leaving Zoey was never easy, and this time was no different. Yet, it *was* different. In some ways it was if he'd staked his claim, made a promise, verified their eventual future. On the other hand, that kiss just made it even harder to say goodbye, and face the seemingly endless days until they could be together for real.

"Hey, give me just a minute, I need to get this." Zach rolled from his position between the pretty blonde's legs so he could answer the phone. Normally he wouldn't have interrupted what promised to be some pretty decent sex for a phone call, but it was Zoey's ringtone and he tried to always answer when she called.

The blonde immediately decided to vie for his attention by playing dirty. Before he had even gotten a single word out, she was on her knees taking him in her mouth.

"Oh, fuck." His breath hissed out just as he slid his finger across the screen to accept the call.

"What? Zach, what's wrong?" Zoey's voice pulled him from his foggy state of horniness.

"Nothing, nothing's wrong. I wasn't talking to you, pretty girl." Zach attempted to collect his thoughts and calm his libido at the same time.

"Pretty girl? You're in bed with me and taking calls from other girls?" The head between his legs popped up and pretty much shrieked the question.

"Zach? What's going on? Are you with girl?" Zoey's hurt blared through the phone.

As he watched the blonde pull her clothes back on and huff out the door, he tried to lie, but nothing came to him quickly enough.

"Not now, I mean, she left, I mean, no, I'm not with anyone." He sighed heavily.

He was in his senior year and the last semester of school promised to be challenging yet fun. He'd kept the edge off with a few girls over the years, but had never really committed to any of them for longer than a week or two at most. He definitely wasn't a total whore like his cousin Kendrick, but an occasional no-strings-attached romp took place now and then. Although, if he was being honest with himself, those romps more-often-than-not were decent blowjobs and nothing more. He just couldn't get around the fact he felt like he was betraying Zoey, and the girls usually caught on pretty quickly that he wasn't exactly emotionally available. He was so ready to be back home in Torey Hope, with Zoey.

"What's up, Zoey Belle? How's school?" Zach tried to sooth her hurt by getting her to talk.

Sighing heavily, she took the bait, but not before getting in her thoughts on the situation. "Zach, I know what we have is special and unique and not the same as other relationships."

She paused, and he pictured her big green eyes watering. "But this really sucks. I just want you home, with me. I don't want to think about how my calls may interrupt your sexcapades. I don't want to keep telling Jason and the other guys that I'm not interested."

When she paused after that statement Zach felt his heart bottom out.

"You don't want to tell them you're not interested? *Are* you interested? Pretty girl, I never wanted to hold you back. I won't let you go easily, and I won't like it at all, but if you want to date other guys it's okay. It's not fair of me to tell you not to. Except, I *will* tell you not to date Jason. He's a douche bag." Zach was adamant.

"No, Zach, that's just it. I *don't* want to date any of them. I'm just so tired of telling them no. I want you here at home so they all will just back off." Zoey's weariness was clear.

"One semester, Zoey Belle, that's all we've got to get through. Then, I'll be home and we can spend all the time together that we want." Zach smiled into the phone thinking about being home and having her by his side.

"Oh! I almost forgot the reason I called. I've been keeping a secret from you until I knew it was all official." She sounded so excited Zach couldn't help but grin.

"I'm not sure I like secrets, Zo. What is it?" There was no way it was a bad secret or she wouldn't have sounded so excited.

"I'm graduating high school a year early. So, when you guys come home, I'll officially be out of school. I'm going to start taking classes here in town so I can become a certified personal trainer, and I'll work at The Center+ when I'm not in class."

"Zoey, I'm so proud of you. I knew you were hella smart, but I didn't realize you'd been doubling up on classes so much that you could skip a whole year."

"Well, I didn't have to do much doubling. I tested out of quite a few. I've been working on getting out early since my eighth grade year, but I just found out today that I officially have all of my classes completed."

"So, let me get this straight. We have about five months and then I'm home doing what I've always dreamed of, and I'll have my favorite girl by my side? This is close to the best day of my life."

"Only *close to* the best day of your life? Gee thanks!" Zoey laughed.

His voice lowered into a whisper, "Close to, because *the best* day of my life will be when I finally get to take you in my arms and kiss you."

He heard her voice catch, "I can't wait for that. I dream of it every day."

"Hey, pretty girl, I've got an early class, so I better go. I'm so proud of you, and I can't wait to be home and living my life with you."

"I love you, Zach."

"Love you too. Still my forever girl?" Zach husked out.

"Always your forever girl."

"ZACH, it's not your usual time to call. Is everything okay?" Her sweet voice filled the air, and he immediately felt more relaxed.

"Yeah, pretty girl, everything is fine. I'm studying for a really hard test, and I just wanted to hear your voice."

She sighed into the phone.

"That's so sweet. I'm glad you called."

"I really can't stay on the phone long, I just needed a five minute break and wanted to talk to you." His voice held an edge of exhaustion.

"Call me anytime. Kick ass and take names on your test." She giggled as she gave him the pep talk.

"Goodnight, pretty girl."

HIS PHONE TRILLED from the bedside table.

Rubbing bleary eyes he tried to focus on the clock.

1:00 a.m. Who would be calling at this time?

Immediately he realized it was Zoey's ringtone. He'd fallen asleep studying for finals. Removing the book from his chest he rolled to the side and snatched his phone.

"Zoey Belle, what's wrong?"

"Hiiiiiii, Zaaaach." A fit of giggles erupted over the phone line.

"Zoey? What's going on? Where are you?"

"I'm with Aly. We're at a par-tay."

"Zoey, are you drinking?"

"Nope." Her lips popped on the *p*.

"Zoey..." His voice held a warning tone.

"Okaaaay, maaaybe I've been drinking just a tiiiiny bit." Another eruption of giggles.

Rubbing his eyes, and trying to think with a level head, Zach got out of bed and walked to Decker's room.

His cousin was up studying. He looked up with a confused look.

Mouthing quietly, Decker asked, "What's up?"

Zach covered the phone and whispered, "Zoey's at a party. She's drinking with Aly. Call your dad and let him know he needs to go get Aly and Zoey. I don't want to call my dad, he and mom will just worry too much. Calling Kyle and Josie may get Zoey in trouble. I think Uncle Nate is the best bet."

In the few seconds it took to tell Decker what was going on Zoey had gotten very quiet on the phone.

"Zoey? Zoey Belle? What are you doing now? Who's with you?" He attempted to keep his voice calm.

"Zach? Zach, I'm so tired of it all. Tired of being the smart girl. Tired of being the hometown girl. Tired of waiting on you to kiss me, like really kiss me." She hiccupped.

"Hey pretty girl, as soon as I'm home, we'll fix that." He worried about her being drunk at a party if she was wanting kisses.

"Zoey, where's this party?" He knew he needed to get an address for his uncle.

"It's at Jason's house. You remember Jason? Cute guy,

wants me for my brains as much as my body." Another giggle and hiccup.

"Can you believe he told me that? Zoey, you're so smart. I'm in love with your brains as much as I'm in love with that tight-ass little body of yours. Yeah, and that's supposed to make me want to date him?" She snorted.

While Zach attempted to control his temper there was muffled talking over the phone.

"Shut up, Aly. He's *not* my cousin." Zoey sounded close to tears.

"Zoey? Hey, why don't you and Aly walk outside and get some fresh air."

Since he'd made it his business long ago to know where Jason lived, he scribbled the address down and handed it to Decker.

"Zach? What if I'm a bad kisser, you only gave me a tiny kiss that one time? Maybe I should let the boys here kiss me for practice. Or sex? What about sex? You've had sex, but I haven't. What if you find out I'm no good at it and you want to give up on me? I should have lots of sex with the boys at this party so I'm good at it by the time you get home. I can spread my legs just as well as these other girls."

A slight beeping sound made its way to Zach's brain as he fought off hyperventilation from what Zoey was saying.

"Zoey, what's that sound, pretty girl?" Zach began to feel even more panicky.

"Beep, beep. It's my battery. It's almost dead. My phone

wants to sleep." A giggle. "Zach, I want to sleep too. I'm so tired." Her voice faded and it sounded like she slid down a wall hitting the floor with a thump.

"Zoey? Zoey Belle? Uncle Nate is coming to get you and Aly. Stay where you are and don't let anyone take you anywhere. Zoey?!"

The line had gone dead.

Cocking his arm back to throw his phone in frustration, he jumped in surprise when a hand grabbed his elbow.

"Man, you don't want to do that." Decker, calm as usual, forced Zach's arm down.

"My dad is about five minutes away from the address you gave me. He's going to stay on the phone and talk to us until he gets there, finds them, and has them safe in his car. You don't want to bust your phone." Decker put his phone on speaker.

Zach paced the room, silently cursing, while the worst of the worst scenes played out in his mind. Zoey would never have said those things if she was sober. But she was drunk, and as far as he knew it was the first time she'd ever been drunk, so there was no telling what decisions she might make. He could only hope Nate found them in time.

About fifteen minutes later he almost wept in relief.

"Hey there Zoey, Aly. Why don't we get in my car and I'll take you both home." Nate's voice came through the phone line.

"There you go, upsy-daisy, I've got you."

Zach could hear the concern in his uncle's voice, but he also noticed he sounded slightly amused.

"Hey, boys, I've got them. They were just sitting on the front porch. There are about ten other kids passed out in the house. I'm going to load the girls up and get them home." Nate filled them in as he helped the girls to the car.

"If they puke in my car, you two are chipping in to pay for the cleaning." Nate chuckled.

"Uncle Nate?" Zoey's miserable voice was heard over the line.

"Yeah, Zoey Belle?"

"I think I'm going to be sick..."

Zoey and Aly spent the next day suffering the consequences of drinking at the party by drowning in severe hangovers. They spent the next two weeks serving their consequences by cleaning the bathrooms at The Center+, even the hair from the shower drains.

5

Zach and his cousins watched as the apartment they had called home for the last four years disappeared from view. Leaving campus for the last time, the four men were nostalgic and, at the same time, excited.

There had been both good and bad times in those four years. But, a day's drive was all that stood between them and their futures. With the U-Haul loaded, and all four piled into Zach's dark red Ford F-150 Raptor, they were grateful their other vehicles had been driven home after graduation by other family members. With four of them on the journey they'd each only have to drive about three hours.

Each man had fond memories of college, but knowing they were headed home to Torey Hope to see their dreams come to fruition, it was easy to catalog the memories under 'good time' and look ahead to bright futures.

Driving through Torey Hope brought smiles to their faces. They'd been home occasionally throughout college, but traveling the streets where they grew up and planned to settle down had them seeing things in a whole new light. As the truck pulled into the driveway of their grandparents John and Cindy Morgan, they each took in the sight before them.

"Aw, man, look; they hung a banner out for us." Sawyer spoke softly.

All four turned to look out the windows of the truck; the words WELCOME HOME blurred slightly in four sets of eyes as they blinked back tears.

The homecoming was emotionally charged, but happier than their other visits through the years because this time they were staying put. Hugs, kisses, and tears flowed abundantly.

After a tear-filled bear hug, Zach patted his father, Nicky, on the back and assured him he wasn't leaving again. Turning at the squeal of delight he heard from behind him, Zach opened his arms to welcome Zoey into them. Picking her up around the waist and swinging her around, he hugged her close. "Zoey Belle, girl, I've missed you so much."

She buried her head in his neck and breathed deep.

"Zach, you have no idea how much I've missed you. I'm so glad you're home, I need you here with me. We can talk about it more later, but I'm just really glad to have you here again." Zach raised a questioning eyebrow at her words, but more welcomes and hugs were being given and the subject was dropped for a while.

After a dinner of Chinese takeout that reminded Zach of the old days, he and Zoey headed out for a walk. They spoke of random things as they meandered through town. Zach had her giggling at his play-by-play of Decker's recent break-up, and Kendrick's sexual escapades during their time away.

They discussed their ideas and plans for sharing the job of fitness instructor at The Center+. Since Zoey had graduated early she was available to teach several classes each week as long as they worked around her college classes.

"I'm so proud of you, Zoey. Graduating early, already working on your degree to become a personal trainer. What types of classes are you taking?" Zach asked, genuinely interested, but also attempting to avoid the emotional tension growing between them.

"Well, I'm either taking or will be taking classes in nutrition, exercise physiology and kinesiology." Zoey took the bait, though Zach knew she recognized his avoidance. "And working at The Center+ will help me because I can earn hours toward my certification. I'm also going to become a certified Pilates instructor; Uncle Nate said the new mixed martial arts instructor he's hoping to hire is also certified in Pilates, so maybe the new guy can help me out."

They reached the local park and slowed in a grove of trees. A huge boulder was positioned perfectly for sitting in a secluded location. Climbing on the rock and patting the seat beside him, Zach invited Zoey to sit.

"So, what will be on your agenda once you get started at work?" Zoey's interest was real, but he knew she was taking her cues from him and avoiding talk of anything serious.

"Well, Decker is going to get an assistant manager hired. All of us are going to work out which classes to offer and schedules; we'll work closely with Mom, Aunt Libby, and Aunt Audrey to get all of that planned. Kendrick will start building the foundation for his sports teams. Sawyer and your mom will be working closely with the new MMA instructor on the new arts program; I'll be assisting with that a lot because we're wanting to combine a lot of the arts and fitness programs. Hopefully you'll be able to attend some meetings and help with decision making." Zach leaned over and bumped her shoulder with his. "I'll also be drumming up funds through our advertising partners as well."

"I want to be involved in as much as I can be. I've been waiting four very long years for you guys to get back here and move The Center+ towards the vision you have for it."

With a slight sigh Zoey leaned her chin and arms on her pulled-up knees.

"What is it, pretty girl?" Zach's fingers grazed her cheek.

"I don't know, it's hard to explain." Zoey whispered.

"Just talk to me, do your best, we'll figure it out together."

"Okay, I'll try." Taking a deep breath Zoey began. "Having you climb out of your truck today, knowing you were home for good was the best feeling in the world. Except it was also the most disappointing and scary moment I've had in a long time."

When Zach's face crinkled in confusion Zoey smiled and continued. "See, I told you it's hard to explain."

"Go on."

"Ever since I hugged you today, I've been trying to pinpoint my uneasiness. For four years I've pinned my every hope and dream on you coming home and us finally being able to be together. Every time I've learned of your dates or more intimate moments I've been able to shake it off because of our age and waiting on this moment. But, now that you're here, I'm worried that we've grown apart. I'm not experienced at all when it comes to boys; I know you didn't ask me to, but I pretty much ignored most other guys because they weren't you. But, you're older, more experienced. Even if you still want to be with me like you promised four years ago, there's no guarantee that we'll be a good match. You've been my best friend and protector since the moment I was born, what if that's all we're meant to be?"

Zoey raised teary eyes to look directly at him before she glanced away.

"I guess, as bad as the four years of waiting were, I could at least pretend everything was going to work out for us. But now that you're home, I have to face the very real possibility that we've drifted away from those long-ago promises."

Moving abruptly so he could pull her close to his chest,

Zach kissed the top of her head. "I hear what you're saying, I do. But, I think you need to know some things before you doubt what we have. Yes, I've had a few sexual encounters between high school and college. More often than not though, I'd settle for oral sex and then feign exhaustion and send the girl on her way."

When Zoey scrunched her brows in confusion, he continued.

"I just never could get into it very much. Do you know why?"

Zoey just shook her head.

"Because I was thinking of a beautiful green-eyed girl keeping my heart warm back in Torey Hope." He wrapped his arms around her tightly and buried his nose in her hair.

"Zoey, I told you that last night in your room, you stole a piece of my heart the moment you wrapped your little hand around my finger. I could no more move on from you, from us, than I could stop breathing. There's no way we won't be a match, we're soul mates, meant to be together."

His finger reached out to gently lift her chin, turning her face to look at him.

"How many kisses have you had, pretty girl?"

As he spoke, his mind and heart were at war.

She's still just seventeen, man. Reel it in.

She'll be eighteen in a very short time, she's mature enough to have a kiss.

Sure, a kiss from someone her age, but not a kiss from a twenty-two year old.

Her next words pulled him from his thoughts and sealed his decision.

"Two or three aside from the one from you, but none of those others were very good. I really didn't see what the big deal is." Her lashes fluttered against her cheeks.

Leaning in, his lips hovering just above her sweet mouth, he whispered, "Well, we'll just have to change that."

His mouth feathered kisses along hers. When his tongue ghosted along her bottom lip, she gasped, and he was done for. Threading both hands into her hair, holding the back of her head, he deepened the kiss.

Her arms came up and snaked around his neck, pulling him closer.

Letting his tongue dance along the seam of her lips, he begged an invitation all the while knowing she'd be smart to stop him before things got too heated on his first night home.

But she didn't stop him. A moan from the back of her throat sounded as she opened to his request. Their tongues played a sweet game of hide-and-seek before he pulled back, holding her face in his large hands and breathing heavily.

Leaning his forehead against hers he spoke gruffly. "Still think kissing isn't a big deal?"

With a sexy smile Zoey bit her bottom lip and shook her head as she blushed.

"No, I think kissing YOU is about the best thing I've ever

done and I want to do it more." She pulled his mouth to hers and kissed him with a passion that had him about to bust out of his boxer briefs.

Quickly pulling back, he slid from the rock and pulled her with him. Settling his back against the weather-roughened surface, he positioned her between his legs and held tightly at her waist.

"Zoey Belle, you've just proven to me that there is no one in this whole world better matched to me than you. But we've got a problem we should talk about."

Her face fell and he raised her chin to look in his eyes.

"Pretty girl, there's nothing we can't get through together, but we *do* need to talk about it. It's sort of the elephant in the room, and it's not going to go away. At least not for a little bit."

She sighed deeply, "My birthday."

"Yes, your birthday. You're seventeen. Even though we've known each other our entire lives, and you know I'd never force you into anything, I don't feel right about it until you're eighteen."

"Zach, I've read the Illinois law several times. The age of consent in Illinois is seventeen, so by law I can consent to a physical relationship with you."

He tweaked her nose, "I've read the law too. More than several times. You're right, the legal age of consent is seventeen. However, it also states that a person eighteen or older, like me, can't engage in sexual acts with someone under eighteen if in a position of authority or trust. I know there's a lot of wiggle room in there, and I know you're not going to press charges against me, but I'd just feel better about everything if we waited. My age, your age, me being a trusted family member, the closeness of our families even though we're not technically related, it's all just too much."

He kissed her again softly, "Besides, I don't think we should fall right into bed. I want to take you out on dates, spend time with you, let 'Zach and Zoey' grow from childhood friends to adults. We've got plenty of time for more. Let's get you to your birthday, then we can play it by ear."

He knew Zoey wasn't happy with his words, but he also knew he wasn't in a hurry. He was back home, Zoey in his arms, family by his side. He didn't care if time stood still.

*O*f course, time didn't stand still.

His cousin Decker and his new girlfriend, who used to be his twin's girlfriend, lived through a chaotic few months with a dangerous, creepy stalker issue.

His cousin Sawyer came out to the whole family, got the crap beat out of him when three homophobic bigots jumped him, and fell in love with Luke, the new martial arts instructor at The Center+.

Zach enjoyed hanging out with Zoey and her brother, Asher. His youngest cousin was right at that stage where he wanted to do everything the older guys were doing, but didn't want to appear like he was a tag-along.

"Hey, are you coming over later to work in the garden with Zoey?" Asher asked, trying to appear nonchalant.

"Yeah, I told her I'd help her out. You going to be there to help share in the misery?" Zach asked. Zoey loved to garden. She still had the great little plot he'd helped her build in her parents' backyard where she could often be found on her knees, elbow-deep in the soil. Zach didn't love gardening, but he knew it made her happy. Plus, she looked adorable in her floppy hat and cute little shorts.

"Sure, I got nothin' better to do so I'll be here." Asher shrugged.

Zach, Zoey, and Asher spent many hours tending her garden and working on projects Asher needed to complete for school.

"You guys want to come over tonight? We'll get pizza and a movie. Invite Aly too." Zach really wanted to spend the evening alone with Zoey, but he knew Asher wanted to come over, and his own sister, Aly, would be bent out of shape if she wasn't invited.

"COME ON, Asher, let's go get the pizza. The girls can stay here and gossip or whatever it is they like to do when we're not around." Zach grabbed his keys and winked at Zoey over Asher's head as they headed toward the door.

Once in the car, Zach could tell Asher was nervous about something.

"What's up, man? You got something on your mind?" Zach tried to be nonchalant.

"I don't know, man. It's just something I've been thinking about, but I don't want to cause problems." Asher blushed.

"Well, we can keep it just between the two of us if you'd rather. But, you can tell me what's on your mind. In fact, I want you to know that you can *always* tell or ask me things. The only time I may have to break confidentiality is if you're involved in something dangerous." Zach knew he could get himself stuck right in the middle of some teen/parent issues, but he also wanted Asher to know he had a friend he could talk to.

"It's just that...I mean...," Asher stuttered around a bit before blurting out, "You like my sister! And I'm having a real hard time getting my head around it."

Zach had often wondered what Asher's take on their relationship was, so he wasn't too caught off guard at the kid's outburst.

"I do like your sister, very much. Just like I like all of my family. But, I'm not going to try to pad my answer around you, you're too smart for that. First, I need you to know something. Do you know that your mom, dad, you, and Zoey are in no way blood-related to my mom, dad, Aly, and me?" Zach figured the cousin thing was weighing on Asher the most.

Asher wrinkled his brow as he thought over the information Zach had just presented.

"What do you mean we're not related? I've known everyone in our family as grandparents, aunts, uncles, and cousins my whole life." Asher obviously doubted Zach.

Pulling over to the side of the road, Zach popped the glove compartment and pulled out a napkin and a pen. He drew a very crude family tree and began labeling it. He knew seeing it doodled out in his notebooks for years had helped him to understand there was no blood relation.

When he finished he handed it to Asher and let the kid do some deducing on his own.

"So, Zoey and I are like second cousins to Decker, Sawyer, Abby, Megan, and Kendrick. But there's no relation between us and you and Aly? Wow, I guess I'd never really thought about it, but you're right."

Asher sat back against the seat and sighed in relief.

"So, you're good with me liking your sister now?" Zach was hopeful.

"I don't know, the guys at school have been giving me a rough time about my *kissing cousins*, but now that I know we're not officially related maybe I can shut them up." Asher shrugged.

"Well, if that doesn't shut them up, you and I can just *happen* by the ball courts sometime and be sure they all have a complete understanding of the matter. Not that it's really any of their business, but I know what it's like to have guys messing with you." Zach glanced at Asher, and noticed the teen wasn't completely relaxed.

"What else is on your mind?" Zach eased the truck back onto the road as he spoke.

"I don't know, I guess I just wonder what happens if you

and Zoey don't work out. I mean, she's my sister, so I sort of have to stick by her side, right? But, does that mean I lose you as a friend?" Asher mumbled in embarrassment.

Zach's heart swelled with pride and love for the kid. He'd missed a lot of Asher's growing up years, but he appeared to have turned into a good kid.

"Well, first, I'm glad to hear you say you'd stick by Zoey's side like any good brother should do. Even when Aly is being a pain in the ass, I love her and stand by her. Although, as I'm standing there, I have to be honest that a lot of the times I'm wanting to kick her ass too." Zach chuckled.

"I hear ya, man. Not so much about *my* sister, but *your* sister truly is a bit of a pain. No offense." Asher added quickly.

"None taken, you speak the truth."

They pulled into the pizza place. Zach handed Asher some money and told him to go pick up the order. Knowing how he used to think it was cool to be trusted to do the same when he was younger he hoped the young man would too.

As they pulled back onto the road, Zach picked up the conversation where they'd ended it earlier.

"On the topic of me and Zoey not working out, I have to tell you I don't think that will be an issue. I've loved that girl since the moment she was born. I know it's hard to understand, and Zoey and I can't even completely explain our connection, but I've known she's the girl for me since before I knew about boy/girl relationships."

He took a deep breath, not wanting to think about a time when he and Zoey weren't together.

"But, if something ever happened to split us up, I need you to know a couple things. One, I would *never* give up on Zoey without a damn hard fight. Two, even if she didn't want to be with me, I would always be here for you. Even though it's not blood-related, we're family and we stick together through thick and thin."

When he looked at Asher he caught the glint of tears in the boy's eyes. As they pulled into the driveway and the truck came to a stop, Zach held a fist out.

"We're cool, no matter what. You got me?"

Asher nodded, swallowing thickly, and bumped his fist against Zach's. "I got you."

Loud voices greeted them when they entered the front door.

"And I'm telling *you*, I'm sick and tired of having to defend what Zach and I have! I love him, he loves me. Even if we were blood-related, which you've known for years we're *not*, I'd still love him. I don't get why you're so against us being happy together. I thought we were best friends!" Zoey's voice was raised to a level Zach hadn't heard it in several years.

He and Asher skirted the room where the girls were having their heated discussion, and proceeded to the kitchen.

"Let's get this all set up, let them yell themselves out, then continue our night." Zach winked at Asher as they began getting ice in glasses.

"Yeah, *best friends*, what a joke! The only reason you were ever willing to hang out with me, from the time we were little bitty until this exact moment right here, is because of Zach! I'm best friend by default, and I always have been. When Zach isn't home, I'm good enough for you. But when he comes home, you drop me like a hot potato and go running to him. The only reason I'm invited here tonight is so my feelings wouldn't be hurt." Aly stopped yelling to catch a breath.

When she continued, it was in a softer, hurt-laced voice. "Admit it, you wouldn't have invited me tonight if you weren't worried about hurting my feelings, would you?"

Aly and Zoey stood facing each other, both breathing a bit heavier from their yelling match. Their heads whipped to the door of the room when Zach and Asher appeared in the doorway.

"Hey ladies, the pizza is ready. Let's eat, then maybe we can talk some things out?" Zach hoped his suggestion would be taken. If the girls started yelling again, he wasn't sure what the next step would be.

They ate an awkward dinner of pizza, chips, apple slices, and soda. Zach had thrown in the apple slices as good measure so any of the parents could rest assured they were getting healthy food.

Zach and Asher attempted to keep the conversation going, but the girls weren't talking much.

When the last bit of pizza was finished and the meal was cleaned up, Zach leaned against the sink. Arms crossed over his chest, he chewed the inside of his cheek as he contemplated the girls.

"Okay, so how are we going to do this? We can all talk together, or separately, but we *are* going to talk because I'm home for good and we're not going to have this tension hanging in the air all the time."

Zach was usually a pretty easy going guy, but he didn't like what his sister was doing. However, he couldn't let on that he was irritated with his sister or all hell would break loose.

Zach watched as Asher signaled he was going to go play video games for a while, and suddenly felt jealous of the kid for getting out of the conversation.

"Oh, yeah, let's let *Zach and Zoey* gang up on me. You two have been excluding me basically since birth, I really don't want to do this right now." Aly blustered as she fought tears.

"Well, you know what? That's just too dang bad, Aly. We *are* going to do this and we're going to do this now. And we'll keep doing this until you get over whatever *this* is." Zoey spoke adamantly.

Walking to the living room, Zach noticed that Zoey smartly chose to sit in a chair away from him.

"Okay, Aly, first I need to say a couple things. One, I'm your brother and I love you. I'll never stop loving you. Two, you know I've loved Zoey since the day she was born, this isn't like a shocking new development. Three, I will continue to love Zoey and make a life with her whether you're on our side or not, but I'd much rather have you with us."

Zach said his piece and then looked to Zoey while Aly attempted to hide her emotions over what her brother had said.

"Aly, we have been friends since before we could even sit up. Our moms have pictures to prove it. Yes, I love Zach and I plan to spend the rest of my life with him, but that doesn't mean I don't love you too. You're not just filler, you're my best girlfriend. No matter how great he is, Zach and I aren't going to giggle over chocolate and magazine quizzes, or get manicures and pedicures while sipping lattes, or hit the mall for mega clearance sales. I choose to spend my time with *you* doing those things because I enjoy my time with you. But, I gotta be honest, Al, right now I'm not enjoying you much at all." Zoey finished her words softly.

"Well, join the crowd, because I'm not enjoying you much at all right now either. I love you, Zoey. And I love my brother. Maybe I am sad we aren't truly cousins? I don't know. But, I get so tired of watching you run off to spend time together. I get it, you have this *fabulous* relationship that no one, not even you, can really explain. But, as an outsider forced to look in, it just sucks."

Aly stood and grabbed her bag. "I want us to work through this, but I think emotions are just too high right now. I'll see you guys later."

When Aly was gone, Zoey curled up on Zach's lap.

"I think she's always been jealous, but I don't know how to fix it. I wish she could see that I can be friends with both of the most important people in my life, I don't have to pick one over another." Zoey sighed deeply.

"I know. I think maybe we just have to give her some time. Maybe make some special plans to spend time with just her?" Zach suggested.

"Part of me thinks that's a good idea, but part of me thinks it just feeds into her immature whiney behavior. I love her, I truly do, but sometimes she makes me so mad." Zoey stopped and looked at him sheepishly. "Sorry, I know it's hard to hear that about your own sister."

"No sorry needed. I'll tell you just like I told Asher: you are only speaking the truth." Zach kissed the top of her head and wondered where this thing with the girls would go.

7

Zach wandered into his sister's room. It had been about a week since her argument with Zoey, and he knew both girls were missing each other.

"Hey, Aly, what's up?" He plopped onto her bed.

"Nothing. What's up with you?" Aly put her e-reader down and looked at her brother.

"Just thought I'd pop in and see how you're doing." Zach hedged a bit, trying to gauge her mood.

"Also thought I'd mention that I know a certain sweet girl is also home today, not doing much, and would probably be up for a visit from her best friend."

"Well then, you better get on over there." Aly snapped.

"Dang it, Al, you know darn well I'm talking about *you* going to see Zoey. You two are about as different as two people can be, but you love each other. I hate to see you fight and throw away a friendship."

"Zach, it's just really hard. I'm so glad to have you home, but now it's like I've become the third wheel all over again. And this time it's worse than before you left because Zoey is old enough to be with you, she's not having to wait, and I'm feeling extremely jealous of what you two have." Aly's eyes welled with tears.

"Aly, you don't need to think of it as losing your friend. I plan to keep Zoey by my side from here on out, you're gaining a sister more than losing a friend. You've always known we were joined at the hip, I really hope you can be happy for us." Zach stood to leave. "Text her and let her know you'd like a quiet evening with her. I'll stay away for tonight."

As her brother left the room, Aly noticed her dad in the hallway.

"What are you doing lurking out there, Daddy?"

Nicky stopped in the doorway, "I'm not lurking, I was just waiting for Zach to leave." He came in and hugged her close.

Sitting next to her on the bed, Nicky was quiet for a moment.

"I know you and Zoey had a fight. I don't like to think of any of my family mad at each other." Nicky's brow furrowed.

"We're not so much mad at each other, we are just having a hard time adjusting to Zach being back home."

"I think you're the one having the hard time. I know

you've gotten used to having Zoey all to yourself for four years, and now you're having to learn to share her with Zach all over again. You're sort of like a baby with a toy, and you don't want to share your toy." Nicky wasn't trying to hurt his daughter, he was just speaking his mind as usual.

"Gee, thanks, Daddy."

"But, you're not a baby anymore. Babies don't understand that it's more fun to play together. You're almost an adult, you should know that you can still have Zoey as a friend even though she's old enough to be with Zach now." Nicky paused. "You should really get used to the idea of sharing your friend before you lose her."

Nicky started to get up, but Aly stopped him.

"Daddy, are you okay with Zach and Zoey being a couple?" Aly cocked her head.

"Yes, I'm okay with it. I don't think real cousins should be in a relationship like that, but they aren't really related. I don't really know why those two have always been so close, but I know you can't help who you love. I don't think Zach could find anyone better for him. And, aside from you and your mom, I'm not sure there's any more special girl than Zoey." Nicky leaned in and kissed his daughter's head.

"I think you should go spend an evening with your friend." Nicky winked and headed down the hall.

Aly grabbed her phone and contemplated sending Zoey a text. In the end, she just grabbed a bag and headed over to the Martin home. She'd been going over there for sleepovers her entire life, she knew she'd be welcomed. Well, at least she hoped she would.

When she arrived, Zoey's father, Kyle, met her at the door.

"Aly, good to see you. What brings you by?" Kyle ushered her into the kitchen.

Aly had to smile at the man. He'd always marched to the beat of a different drummer, yet was one of the most down-to-earth, soft-hearted men she'd ever met. On this day, his hair was dyed multi-colors and swept all to one side of his head. She admired the newest tattoo on his arm.

"I didn't know you'd gotten new ink. I swear, I can't wait until I turn eighteen so I can have you do my first tattoo." Aly smiled as Kyle rolled his eyes.

"Well, you get permission from your parents, I need to know Nicky won't hold it against me. Then we'll get something set up."

Aly's eyes were drawn to the backyard where she saw her best friend digging in her garden.

Kyle noticed where Aly had looked. "She's missing you. She's a stubborn one and won't admit it, but she doesn't like not having you around."

"Well, I think we're probably both a little bit too stubborn for our own good." Aly sighed.

"She'll probably be out there for a bit longer. Would you like to hear a story?" Kyle offered.

"A story? Well, I'm not exactly a child anymore, but sure I'll listen to your story." Aly smirked.

"This isn't a children's story, Aly. This is a very real-life story with a powerful lesson. I'm telling it to you in hopes of saving you some of the heartache I went through." Kyle handed Aly a bottle of water, and then settled against the sink to tell his tale.

"I was in love with a girl named Isabelle. I called her Izzy B. She was a rebel, just like me. We fell in love from the first moment we met as children. We grew up together, forever in love. I married that girl, my Izzy. We were happy, we were best friends. And then, for reasons I will never understand, she was ripped from my life and I sank into a darkness I thought I'd never be able to fight my way through."

Kyle paused to take a drink.

Aly knew Kyle was married before Josie, but she'd never heard the details. Her heart hurt for his loss.

"But, I moved to Torey Hope to live with Jeremiah and Audrey, and I met Josie. I was in so much pain. I never wanted to forget Izzy or move on from her. I thought if I ever let myself love someone else it was like I was giving up on the first girl I ever loved, the girl I pledged my heart to. But, over time, thanks to the love and support of friends and family and Izzy herself, I realized I could love in many different capacities. I can love my parents, my friends, and my children in different, but equal, ways. Just like I can love Josie without forgetting Izzy." Kyle gazed out the window and watched his daughter work in her garden.

"That girl out there is my heart and soul. Yes, she's stubborn. But she's also capable of loving several people in several separate but equal ways. She's got a big heart and plenty of love to go around. Just because she's in love with that brother of yours doesn't mean she can't love you too. Let her show you; let her love you; don't fight it. She's got it in her to love you both, no worries." Kyle pulled a teary Aly into a hug.

"Kyle, are you okay with Zoey being with my brother?"

"Aly, I'm as okay with it as a father can be. Do I want to think about the intimate details of your brother and my baby girl? Hell no. But, do I know that Zach would lay down his life for that girl just the same as I would? Yes, I know that with all of my heart. I have never understood their connection to each other, but there's no denying they have something special. If I had to pick a man to love my daughter, I could think of no one better suited for the job than Zach."

They shared one last hug as Zoey cleaned up her tools in the garden and washed her hands.

When she entered the kitchen and found Aly talking to her dad, she smiled warily.

"Hey, girl. What's up?"

"Not much, just thought I'd come over and hang out. If you're not busy?" Aly offered timidly.

"Nah, I'm all yours. Let me shower and then we can plan

the evening." Walking to her father, Zoey kissed his cheek and asked a silent question with her eyes.

"Hey there, Zoey Belle. You and Aly have fun tonight, huh? Let's just not have a repeat of the drinking episode. Unless you both are feeling the need to pull bathroom duty at The Center+ again?" Kyle winked at the girls.

Leaning in to kiss his daughter's cheek, he whispered, "I just reminded her that people can love more than one at a time, you just need to prove it to her."

The girls spent their evening talking, giggling, and eating junk. But there was a tension between them, an elephant in the room.

Zoey didn't bring up the subject of Zach and neither did Aly. She wanted the night to be just them; they could always discuss the argument and their feelings later. But the thing about putting tough conversations off until later is that life sometimes gets in the way.

8

"There's my favorite girl." Zach walked into the studio at The Center+ to find Zoey straightening things up after her last pilates class. He glanced around to be sure no one was watching them, then pulled her into his arms and shuffled them around the corner into the dressing room. His mouth brushed hers lightly as his arms tightened around her.

"Do you know how many years I've dreamed of being able to take you in my arms and kiss you? Now that I can, I don't think I'll ever be able to stop." He caught her giggle with his kiss and pulled her close.

Zoey ran her hands through his hair and smiled, her eyes bright, "That's good, because I don't think I ever want you to stop." She pulled his head down so his lips could meet hers again. The kiss started sweet, but quickly reached a fevered pitch. Zoey groaned as his tongue slipped past her lips. He let his hands travel under her form-fitting shirt, sparks flying when skin met skin.

Knowing he should stop, knowing he couldn't let the kiss go any further, Zach let his lips linger for a few moments longer and willed the evidence of his desire to stop nudging Zoey's abdomen.

Before he could think of anything to calm himself down, Zoey reached down and palmed him in her tiny hand.

Biting her lip and turning emerald eyes up to meet his, she whispered, "I may not have any practice with what to do when I finally get my hands on you, but I sure am looking forward to learning."

The little imp had brought him roaring back to life, and he growled before taking her mouth with his again. Rocking his erection against her hand, he ground out against her ear, "And I can't wait to give you lessons, but based on what you've got me feeling right now, I think you'll be a very quick learner." His head dipped to taste her mouth again, but their moment was shattered.

"Shit! What the fuckin' fuck?! My eyes, my eyes!" Kendrick came around the corner to find them hidden away. After his little outburst, he held his hands over his eyes and pretended to be blind. "Quick, someone get the bleach, my eyes must be bleached if I'm ever to regain my sight." He continued walking into walls and bouncing off of them as he spoke.

"Haha, fucker. Yeah, you caught us, knock that shit off." Zach punched his cousin in the arm. "I don't know why you're acting so surprised, you've been on me for months about what was going on with me and Zoey."

Pretending to peek from behind his hands, Kendrick winced when he saw Zach still held Zoey in his arms. "Giving you shit about something and actually *seeing* what I suspected for a while are two very different things. My poor innocent mind may never recover from what I just saw. One of my best friends, my cousin, shoving his tongue down the throat of my dear Zoey Belle."

Walking over to the couple, Kendrick pulled Zoey close and ran his hands over her as if checking for injuries. "Zoey, talk to me, are you okay? Did he hurt you? How ever did you fight off his tongue?"

When Zoey giggled and slapped at his hands, Kendrick laughed and stepped away.

"All joking aside, I'm happy for you guys." Kendrick looked around as if noticing the three of them were hidden in a corner. "I take it I'm the first to have seen a Zach and Zoey make out session?"

Zach nodded and pulled Zoey protectively to his chest. "It's not that we're denying we're a couple, we just aren't letting others see us physically together until after Zoey's birthday, especially here at work or in public. Around family is a bit different."

"Well, there's no denying you two are a couple; you've been a couple since Zoey was still taking shits in her diaper."

Kendrick winked at her when she groaned in protest of his description. "But, yeah you and Jail Bait better keep this all on the down low. Don't want any rumors or issues cropping up."

Kendrick took a glance towards Zach's zipper, "Speaking of that...dude, you better get the problem *cropping up* in your pants to get *down low* before we head into the meeting."

Zach rolled his eyes and Zoey snickered.

"Zoey, you joining in the meeting? I think it would be good to have your input since you're working here almost full time now." Kendrick held out his arm to her.

Zach nodded to her. "Go ahead with Kendrick, I'm going to take a minute to make myself presentable." He smirked at them and rolled his eyes again as he watched his favorite girl walk away with one of his very best friends. Kendrick was crude, and crass, and crazy; you never knew what would come out of his mouth, but he was also genuine, loyal, and protective. Zach knew he couldn't ask for a better friend or cousin.

When he walked into the small men's locker room just off the studio, he was too preoccupied with thoughts of Zoey to notice a shadowy figure behind the door. No one saw the figure slip from the locker room and out the side exit of The

Center+. And no one saw the hatred that filled the man's face.

THE MEETING RAN AS usual with all the main people there. Jeremiah Jordan and Nate Morgan had accepted more silent roles since the four younger men had come back to Torey Hope to run The Center+. Decker Morgan ran the meeting with help from his assistant manager, Katie Turner.

Josie and Sawyer and Luke spoke to the group about the arts programs, what was running well, what needed a little more publicity, and what was on the agenda later on down the road. They welcomed Zoey into the group, and thanked her for her dedication to the classes she'd been teaching. Zoey took a brief moment to tell them about things she had in mind to expand the fitness programs as she continued to take classes and work toward becoming a physical trainer.

Kendrick had spent much of the months they'd been back in town scouting out players, putting out feelers with the local coaches in Torey Hope and surrounding communities, and building his sports programs. He'd get things started with football, then a basketball program, and he'd round out for the time being with baseball. The hope would be these programs would run during the off seasons and also provide extra skill work during the seasons so The Center+ would have an excellent feeder program to build the local and regional school sports programs. He had his coaches and assistant coaches hired, and they were all itching to get things started.

Zach took a moment to speak to the group about the advertising successes they'd had recently, what was working, what needed tweaked, and what he had planned. When the boys came back to Torey Hope, The Center already had a couple large financial backers, but the cousins had immediately pulled a couple more supporters on board, changed the name to The Center+, and were now looking at three other lucrative deals which would keep the business afloat for several years to come.

With the meeting over and no other classes to teach, Zoey was done for the day. Zach had been counting on her finishing up early because he had plans for their next couple days.

When she walked into his office, he immediately closed the door and gathered her in his arms. "If I'm dreaming, I don't want to wake up. Having you sitting in meetings with me while I do what I love is beyond a dream come true. Having you walk into my office and me be able to hold you and kiss you is perfection." He leaned in and kissed her lips softly.

Pulling back, he smiled at her. "Please tell me you don't have any plans this weekend."

"I don't have any plans this weekend." Zoey mimicked.

"Little smart ass." He tweaked her nose.

"Well, that's good, because we are going to spend the

entire weekend together. I've already cleared it with Decker so we don't have to be here all weekend. And, I took it upon myself to clear it with your parents too."

Zoey's eyes grew round and her mouth dropped into a little O.

He reached up and gently closed her mouth. "No worries, pretty girl."

"What did they say when you said you wanted to spend the weekend with me?"

"Well, your mom blushed and smiled at your dad. Then your dad tried to look tough, but he finally just cracked up laughing and said, 'I can't even attempt to be angry. I know you love our girl, and we know you'd never do anything to hurt her. Just remember she's a lot younger than you. We trust you both, don't do anything to lose that trust.'"

"Wow, nothing like laying on the guilt, huh?" Zoey smirked.

"Yeah, well, they're right. I don't ever want to hurt you or lose your or their trust." He kissed her again.

"Go home, pack for the weekend, and I'll be there to pick you up in an hour. You'll need comfortable clothes, workout clothes, and clothes you don't care if they get dirty. Bring a nicer outfit too. Oh, and sunscreen. Wouldn't want you to get that pretty little nose burned."

He tapped her nose, kissed her cheek, and ushered her out the door. "One hour. Be ready."

Zoey looked at him, smiling. "This is really happening,

isn't it? You're home, we're together, and we finally get to be Zach and Zoey the couple instead of the friends."

She leaned in and whispered, "I know this is usually saved for a huge dramatic announcement, but for us it's the way it's always been. I love you, Zachary Malone Morgan." She kissed him quickly, and then waved her fingers at him as she walked away.

He shut the door, leaned against the door, closed his eyes, and sighed. "I love you too, Zoey Belle."

Zoey climbed into Zach's dark red Ford F150 truck, and he shut the door behind her before walking to his own side to climb in. He'd always opened doors for females, his mom and dad had taught him that at a young age, but being able to open the door for Zoey as *his* girl meant more.

She bounced excitedly on the seat.

"You seem pretty hyped up, pretty girl." Zach laughed at her. "We aren't flying to Paris or anything."

He reached over and pulled her close to his side. Leaning in to kiss her head, he whispered, "Someday I'll take you somewhere exotic. Promise."

She pushed away from him slightly and cocked her head. "Zach, you know I don't need exotic locations, I just need to be near you. If you told me right now that you were taking me to the gas station for a fountain soda pop and candy bar, I'd be thrilled. Just being with you is all that matters to me."

She kissed his cheek, "Please don't ever forget that."

He turned and caught her lips in his. Bringing his hand up to cup the back of her head, he angled her for better access. The heat which grew between them threatened to end the trip before it even left the driveway.

A loud knock on the window had them jumping like they'd been shocked with a hot poker. Zoey screamed and then laughed, hiding her head in Zach's shoulder.

Zach, fearing who was at the window of his truck, turned slowly while his cheeks tinted pink.

When he found both Kyle and Josie standing at his driver side with their eyebrows raised, he slowly rolled the window down.

And waited.

Waited for what seemed like ages before one of them spoke.

"Are you two planning on going on your little trip or are you just going to make out in my driveway? I gotta tell you, if you're just going to make out I may have to rescind my blessing on this trip. I won't spoil your surprise, but you told me this wasn't just an excuse to get Zoey alone with you, and I believed you. Does that still stand?" Kyle wasn't truly mad, everyone could tell that, but he did look a little put off by finding his daughter with Zach's tongue halfway down her throat.

"Yes, sir. I still have the same plans I told you about. I appreciate you not ruining the surprises I have for our girl here. I assure you, nothing more than what you saw is planned for this weekend. I'm sorry, I know it's got to be hard to see us go from best friends to something more. But, you've got to know that I love this girl with my entire being, always have, always will. We've waited for so long for our ages to be more appropriate, we just got a little overwhelmed and caught up just now."

Zach was being genuine and he didn't come across as patronizing or smarmy, but everyone saw exactly why Zach was such a good advertising agent within The Center+. The guy could sell ice to Eskimos.

"Sorry, Daddy, Momma. We'll be good, promise. You know I've been counting down the days until I can call Zach my boyfriend. Having him home and *mine* is a dream come true. Thank you for allowing us to have this weekend."

Zoey was five years younger than him, but she was more mature than most girls her age. He grasped her hand.

"So, if you're okay with it, we're going to head out. We've got destination numero uno to reach tonight. If we time it right we'll get there with about two hours left before closing time." Zach looked askance at the couple he'd considered family his entire life.

"One last question. The sleeping arrangements..." Kyle trailed off when Josie clasped his hand in hers. "You know what, on second thought, I don't want to know. I trust my daughter and I trust you. I don't want to ask something that makes either of you lie, so I'll pretend like I know nothing. Josie here will keep me busy doing all kinds of kinky things tonight so I don't have to think about what the two of you are doing."

He wagged his eyebrows and smiled as Zach laughed, Zoey groaned, and Josie playfully smacked his arm.

The big truck backed slowly out of the driveway and headed toward the next town over.

"Are you going to tell me where we're going?" Zoey asked.

"Now, what would be the fun in that?" Zach smiled at her pout. "We'll be there in about thirty minutes. I think you can wait until then."

The entire half-hour drive was filled with laughter and chit-chat. Zach realized that nothing had changed between them. It was like they were four years prior, she had always been his best friend, and she still was. The only difference was he'd gone from someday wanting to kiss her, when the time was right, to being able to hold her and kiss her anytime he wanted. But, other than that small tidbit, she was still his favorite forever girl. His heart warmed.

"So, speaking of sleeping arrangements. I planned on doing whatever you thought would be best. We can get completely separate rooms, one room with two beds, or just one bed. It's your decision, but either way I don't want anything going too far tonight. Your birthday is so close, then after that we can start talking about the next steps." Zach knew she was disappointed, so he reached over and lifted her chin so she was looking in his eyes.

"Zoey Belle, the first time I make love to you isn't going to be in a hotel room. It isn't going to be an afterthought or mistake. I'm not going to back down on that. I love you, I've always loved you, I will always love you. But, I'm determined that if we've waited this long, we can wait until you're 100% legal and do it right." He leaned in and kissed her before entwining his fingers with hers. "But that doesn't mean that I'd be against holding you close while we sleep tonight."

"Okay, Zach. I know where you're coming from, and I know you're right. It doesn't diminish how much I want you, how badly I want to feel what it's like to be with you that way, but I'll settle for whatever we can get. Let's get one room, one bed. You can hold me all night long." She leaned into his body and breathed deeply.

"Pretty girl, I'll hold you all night long, and for the rest of our lives. That's a promise."

They arrived at the zoo.

Zoey looked at him confused. "Zach, I think the zoo is only open at night on certain dates. It doesn't look like it's open this evening." She looked like she felt bad for him.

"You're right, the *zoo* isn't open tonight, but the butterfly garden is. And, if the lady I talked to on the phone is right, we should see some butterflies hatching this evening."

"Zach, this is so neat. I've lived close to this exhibit since it opened five years ago, but I've never taken the time to come over to see it. Thank you. You know what a sucker I am for butterflies and flowers." She smiled sweetly at him and kissed him lightly.

They walked the short distance to the entrance. Once Zach had paid their entry fee and the price for both of them to feed the butterflies, they walked into a tropical oasis filled with lush plants and flowers and over 100 species of butterflies.

For the next two hours, Zoey was in heaven. Zach couldn't have cared less for the plants and insects, but watching his girl enjoy the evening was his own little spot in paradise.

"We *have* to come back here sometime. I think the grandmas and moms would enjoy this too. I can't believe there are so many different types of butterflies. I wish I could grow some of these plants, but I am definitely planting a butterfly bush so the backyard will be full of them this summer." Zoey babbled on as she gazed at the beautiful vegetation, and giggled when the light tickle of butterfly wings danced along her skin.

All too soon, the clock struck closing time.

"Come on, pretty girl, we need to let the butterflies get their sleep." He had let her wander the gardens freely, but grasped her hand in his and pulled her close to his side as they walked out the door.

Stopping in the protected area between the inner and

outer doors, they let an employee check them over to be sure they weren't carrying any stowaways with them.

"Oops, you've got one trying to make an escape here on your shoulder. If you'll just hold still a moment, I'll get him off and back into his home." The employee made a move to gently remove the butterfly.

The insect fluttered from Zoey's shoulder to her hand.

"Oh, Zach, look how pretty it is. It's the biggest one I've seen. He's gorgeous." The awe in her voice filled the small area.

As if pushed by a whisper of breeze, the butterfly zigged and zagged around Zoey's strawberry-blonde hair before lighting on her nose.

Trying her best to stay still so as not to startle the gentle creature, a breathy giggle escaped her.

Zach's heart filled, his breath caught in his chest. He would keep the image of her giggling with a butterfly on her nose in his heart for the rest of his life. Never once had he doubted the girl standing in front of him was his soulmate, and watching her smile as if the winged insect was the most precious thing in the world cemented her place in his heart and soul.

Once the tagalong had been safely returned to his garden home, they walked out into the evening. Arriving at his truck, Zach quickly gathered her in his arms and pressed her back against the shadowed driver's side away from onlookers. Running a gentle hand across her cheek, he swallowed audibly when her sparkling emerald eyes lifted to meet his own.

"Zach?" She whispered, her chest rising and falling quickly.

"You are the most beautiful, special, amazing woman I've ever known. I don't know how or why watching you in there affected me so strongly, but it did." He stopped speaking and slowly lowered his mouth to hers.

This kiss was different. This kiss was a promise of something more to come, and Zoey felt the heat sear through her body. When she thought her heart would explode, he stumbled backwards breathing heavily.

"Zoey..." With fire in his eyes, he reached for her again, but simply pulled her into his chest. Allowing their breathing to return to normal, they stood in the shadows of the evening.

"We need to go somewhere, anywhere, but not to the hotel just yet. Let's get some supper or dessert at least. I can't be in a hotel with you right now." He adjusted himself as he spoke and his eyes twinkled at his girl's flushed cheeks and swollen lips.

"I think there's nothing I want more than to find a hotel right this moment." She quipped.

"Hey, sassy pants, don't tempt me. There's nothing more I want right now either, but that's not what this weekend is about. We both need to cool down before we climb in bed." He tapped her nose and kissed her gently. "Come on, let's get out of here."

As they drove away, Zoey sighed and watched the butterfly garden fade in the distance.

"Well, tonight was special from the moment we arrived, but that kiss just put the evening into my Top Five best dates ever." She looked at him and smiled.

"Only in the top five? Which dates were better? And since I've not taken you on many dates, you better not tell me about dates with other guys." Zach teased her.

"Well, for now, it fills the number one spot. But we've got a whole weekend ahead of us, so we'll see if it can hold onto its ranking." She teased him back.

"Wow, the pressure is on." He chuckled as he opened her door and slowly let her body slide down his as he huskily whispered, "I look forward to the challenge of filling all of your slots." He threw his head back and laughed at the look on her face.

"Oh my gosh, you just sounded so much like Kendrick!" She laughed and threw her arms around his neck.

Her voice whispered in his ear and the heat instantly returned, "You can fill any and every slot you'd like."

He growled into her mouth as he kissed her.

"Pretty girl, you're making things very hard with your teasing." He let his heat press against her belly.

"Hard is just the way I like it." She tried to say it seriously, but dropping sexual innuendos was so foreign to her she couldn't help but to crack up laughing.

Walking into the little coffee shop, they worked hard to control their laughter.

Had either of them seen the lone figure who watched them from a corner booth, their laughter would have died instantly. His angry heated eyes watched silently. Hatred and lust filled him. He had plans for the girl, and her dickhead boyfriend wasn't in those plans.

9

*Z*ach laid on the hotel bed, face down, and groaned into the pillow. He tried to clear his head and get rid of the hard-on he'd had since Zoey disappeared into the bathroom. But he could smell the scent of her body wash wafting on the steamy air under the closed door. He could hear her humming a random song. He could picture her naked body under the hot spray of water. None of those things were helping him to get himself under control.

What the hell was I thinking? I just paid $100 for a night of pure torture. He knew the thought running through his mind was complete truth, but he also knew there would never be a sweeter more satisfying torture. *You're a glutton for punishment, man.* He smiled. Yeah, he was. But if holding his favorite girl all night long was punishment, he never wanted it to end.

The bathroom door opened.

He heard her feet pad over to where he was on the bed.

The bed sank with her weight and he felt the heat from her body.

Zach bounded from the bed and raced the bathroom, "Um, I need to shower," he mumbled as he closed the door.

Shit. He knew he couldn't lay on the bed with her right then, but walking into the steamy, fragrant bathroom where he knew she'd just been naked didn't help matters either.

"Zach? You okay?" She knocked lightly on the door.

"Yeah, I just wanted to get a shower real quick. I'll be out in a bit." As he spoke he almost hoped she'd fall asleep before he finished.

"Okay, well I'm going to watch some TV for a while."

He ran his hands over his face.

His girl was lying in bed waiting for him. And he was behind the bathroom door deciding if he should jack off in the shower just to take the edge off. *Double shit.*

Several minutes later, shivering from the cold shower he'd submitted himself to, he climbed from the shower feeling more confident about sharing a bed with Zoey and keeping her virtue safe.

Until he walked from the bathroom into the darkened room and found his precious girl wide-eyed, slack-jawed, staring at two very naked bodies on the TV screen.

"Zoey? Whatcha doin', pretty girl?" His voice was soft and husky. Holy fuck, she's watching porn. I'm going to die tonight.

I'll bleed out when my balls explode. She has no fucking idea what she does to me.

Her incredulous face turned to him, eyes still wide. "Well, it looks like there's a free weekend on this channel. I didn't realize it was *this* type of channel, but I've never watched porn and I couldn't help but want to see what happens."

She hid her face in her hands. "I mean, I *know* what *happens*, I just couldn't stop watching."

He didn't even attempt to hide the tent in his basketball shorts, it was pointless. Crawling up the bed, he met her at the pillows. He settled his back against the head board and positioned her between his legs so her back rested against his chest. His voice rumbled through his chest as he whispered in her ear, "We can watch anything you want."

She turned and grinned at him, "Can I make mental notes of things I want to try?"

Fuck. Yep, she was trying to kill him.

He chuckled. "Sure, make all the mental notes you'd like. I'll do my best to accommodate your wish list."

They settled in to watch what turned out to be a very soft porn video. And for that he was extremely thankful. He didn't want his girl watching anything too hardcore.

His hands ached to roam her body, but he kept his arms wrapped around her midsection.

When the credits rolled, she turned in his arms.

"I know we can't go too far, but can we mess around just a

little?" Her sweet words were whispered desperately against his lips.

And with that one simple request, he knew he was a goner.

"What did you have in mind, pretty girl?" His mouth spoke huskily against her ear.

With huge, innocent eyes she spoke softly, "I really have no idea. I mean, I know what sex is, and I know we're not doing that tonight. But, I was hoping you could show me a little bit about all that leads up to the actual sex."

She pulled her bottom lip between her teeth and ducked her head embarrassed.

A finger lifted her chin and he spoke gruffly, "Two things, Zoey. First, don't ever be embarrassed to talk to me like this. I need to know what's going on in that sexy, smart head of yours. Two, you're right, we aren't going to have sex, but I'd be more than happy to show you some previews of what we can do once your birthday gets here."

His lips captured hers gently. When his tongue danced across her bottom lip, he took advantage of her gasp and found his way inside. Her hands fisted in his hair as she rolled and pulled his weight on top of her.

"Show me."

The soft whisper floated on the air and his heart clawed its way into his throat.

Bringing his hands up to cup her face, he kissed her deeply before whispering, "I love you, Zoey Belle, always have, always will. Don't ever forget that. This has never been about just sex for me, please don't let tonight change that."

His ragged voice and pleading eyes begged her.

"Zach, if this was about just sex we would have never made it to where we are. Just sex doesn't wait for the perfect forever. Just sex doesn't hold another's heart for almost eighteen years. We will never be just sex."

She leaned up to kiss him, "But, that doesn't mean I don't want to see what the 'almost sex' side of us can get into." She grinned and he couldn't help but laugh.

Their laughter subsided quickly as his hot mouth trailed kisses down her body.

Goosebumps formed under his hands as he slowly traced his fingers along the soft skin of her abdomen. Allowing his hands to roam farther under her tank top, he stopped momentarily to rest his forehead on her ribcage. Shallow breaths escaped him, his mind racing a thousand miles a minute.

"Zach?" She propped up on her elbows and watched him. "What's wrong?"

Tracing her soft skin with his tongue, kissing each rib, he lifted his head, and gazed at her with fiery eyes.

"Nothing is wrong, Zo. I'm just a little overwhelmed. I feel like I've waited for this moment my entire life. I know that's not really true, but I've wanted you to be *mine* in every imaginable way for so long, it's enough to take my breath away to have you here with me like this." Swallowing thickly, he continued, "I'm getting ready to touch you in ways we've never shared, in ways you've never been touched, and I'm feeling a little off-kilter to be honest with you."

"Show me. Please." She pulled the hem of her tank over her head.

With a shaky breath, he sat on his knees between her legs and pulled her close. Fire and water mixed in his heated eyes as he let his tear-glistened gaze roam over her bare skin.

"You are beyond beautiful, beyond breathtaking." His voice caught in his throat as he spoke.

Bringing a hand to her midsection, he let his fingers brush over her skin.

"I'm scared, Zoey. Scared that once I touch you, this will all go away, like I'll find out it's all been one big dream." He fought the tears through his whisper.

"It's not a dream, Zach. I'm here. I love you. And I want you to touch me. Please." She reached for his hand and placed it on her chest.

Closing his eyes, he groaned, and let both hands caress over her bare breasts.

Leaning his body down, and pressing his weight into her, he took her mouth with his. Tongue and lips worked together to taste and tease. Nothing could have prepared him for what he felt when he held her in such an intimate way.

Breathless whimpers, rolling hips, fists gripping sheets, he loved on her for a moment longer before his lips began to journey down her body.

"Zach. Wait."

The words froze his movement and his blood at the same time.

"Do we need to stop, Zo?" He never wanted to do anything that made her uncomfortable.

"Is it weird? Too much? Not what you had hoped for?" He knew then and there, he would never be fit for another after having a taste of her, but he would let her go if she was uncomfortable.

"No, no, not at all. That's just it. I've been scared that once we started this next step, it would get awkward. Aly kept telling me that your kisses and touches would feel wrong, like a brother kissing his sister. And, even though I wanted her to be wrong more than anything, I worried it would all feel strange when we finally came to this. And I was scared to death of how we would deal with it."

She reached out and pulled his hands back to cover her breasts. "But nothing about what we're doing feels wrong or strange. You light my body on fire, like it's come alive for the first time in my life."

She gripped the base of his neck and pulled him close for a deep kiss.

"Show me more." With a final flick of her tongue she arched her back when his lips left hers and traveled down to the waistband of her shorts.

"Is this okay, Zo?" He traced the elastic and kept himself from yanking the shorts down her gorgeous bare legs.

She answered wordlessly, lifting her hips so he could drag

the material of her shorts and panties off her body.

His large hands gripped her hips, and his thumbs caressed along the delicate skin. Breathing hard, he dropped kisses to her navel.

"I think you have too many clothes on." She grinned at him and yanked on his shirt.

"Only my shirt comes off. I need to keep something between us for now." He smiled at her huff of annoyance.

"I'm trying to be good here, Zo. The shorts stay on." He tweaked her nose as he removed his shirt.

"As much as I want to have you show me all about sex. I could beg you while you're completely naked and you'd never take advantage of me, would you?" The love and adoration she had for him was clear in her words and eyes.

"Never. You're too precious to me to screw this up. We'll enjoy each other tonight..." He adjusted himself dramatically, "No matter how *hard* it is to keep that promise."

She giggled, but stopped almost immediately.

"Show me, Zach. Show me what it's all about."

He let his fingers trail along her flesh until he found her warm and wet.

Before she had descended from her first, his mouth found her and her second release barreled through her body.

Pulling her into his arms, he brushed kisses along her neck.

"That was beautiful. You feel okay?" He murmured in her car.

"I feel amazing. That was amazing. If I wasn't so tired, I'd be asking to do it again." She blushed at her admission.

"It can be arranged." Zach winked.

"No, it's my turn now." Zoey rolled over, and straddled his thighs.

"Zoey, no. Tonight was about showing you how good it could be. It's not about me."

His protest fell on deaf ears.

"I said I wanted to know all about what leads up to sex. I want to experience it *all*." She smiled cheekily, waggled her brows, and began to pull his shorts down.

When she succeeded in removing the material completely, she sat back on his thighs and admired him laid out in front of her.

When she licked her lips lightly, he groaned and laughed.

"Like what you see, pretty girl? You look like you're about to devour me." He knew she had no experience with giving or receiving oral sex, but just the thought of her touch on his skin was enough for him to tap out before the fun even started.

"You're beautiful. And very big."

"Big is good, beautiful is not the word most guys are looking for, but if you think I'm beautiful, then it's all good with me."

"Can I touch you?" Her question was soft and uncertain.

"You can do anything or nothing or a mix of the two. I can't promise how long I can last, but you're welcome to touch or watch or just talk." He submitted to her sexy curiosity by placing his hands behind his head.

When her soft, delicate fingers brushed along his length, he knew he had died and gone to heaven. When her tiny fist gripped him and stroked top to bottom and back, he knew he never wanted to return.

"I want to taste you, like you did me."

The strangled moan from him was answer enough.

He had to bring his hands down to clutch the sheets when her warm, wet mouth closed around him. "Oh, damn, Zoey."

"Is it bad? Do you want me to stop?" She licked her lips as she took her mouth off him.

"Oh, hell no. I don't want you to ever stop." He threw his head back as her mouth took him in again.

It wasn't the best blowjob he'd ever received, but it would forever and always be top of his list from that moment on because it was his favorite girl blurring in his vision as he watched her head bob up and down.

"Oh, hell, Zoey. I'm not going to last long. If you don't want me to come in your mouth, you need to stop."

The negative response she hummed against his length took him over the top. He groaned his release and fought the desire to yank her hair and drive into her mouth.

When she pulled off him, and wiped her lips with the back of her hand, he felt like he was going to pass out.

Gathering her in his arms, they curled together and fell

asleep.

HE WAS ON FIRE. He was dying. And it was the best death possible.

He came awake slowly. Recognition dawning on him as he realized Zoey was no longer curled in his arms, but had her hot little mouth on him.

"Damn, Zo, you better be careful, or I may start thinking I need to wake up this way every day." He fought the urge to pump his hips.

"I know Kendrick is adventurous, but I don't think even he would help you with this type of wakeup call." Her quip was teasing before she took him in again.

Laughing as her heat threatened to push him over the edge, he grabbed her quickly and rolled her to her back.

Laying himself between her legs, he tortured himself by pressing into her heat.

"Oh, God, Zach. Please." She rolled her hips against him, begging.

"Not today, but soon, pretty girl." He rocked against her, marveling at how perfectly his body molded to hers. "Someday I'll be right here, nothing between us, and I'll fill your gorgeous body. There is nothing I want more than to make love to you."

When his length connected with her core again, she

bucked against him, whimpering.

"Until then, how about I help you out a bit? Would you like that?" He nipped at her lips, her neck, her ear.

Wordlessly, she grasped his backside and pulled him closer into her.

"Tell me, pretty girl, what do you want?" He teased.

"Touch me, Zach. Taste me." She writhed under him.

He was happy to comply.

LATER, as they washed each other in the shower, Zoey pouted.

"I wanted to make you happy waking you up that way, but you took over and made me crazy. You didn't get anything out of it." She stroked him lightly, huge green eyes gazing up at him.

"Zo, I've never been happier to wake up than I was this morning. Just knowing I had you in my arms would have made me happy, but finding you doing *that* was ecstasy. I may not have come, but I had the pleasure of watching you and knowing it was because of me. Believe me, I got plenty out of it." He let his lips linger on hers, before resting his forehead on hers.

When she dropped to her knees, he hissed out a breath as her mouth closed around him.

He had no problem with her finishing what she'd started.

"So you made me wear workout clothes, what exactly do you have planned for us, Mr. Morgan?" Zoey's eyes twinkled over her French toast breakfast.

"Zoey Belle, when will you figure out that I will *never* tell you my secret plans? One, because it's a secret, and two, because I know it drives you insane."

He smiled at her over his coffee. "All I can tell you is that we are going to the park, we need to be there in about 45 minutes, and I think you will love what we're doing. In fact, the whole reason I wanted you to come do it is because I think you'll want to take it back to The Center+."

She pursed her lips at him and scowled, but he could see she was intrigued by what they were going to be doing.

Thirty-five minutes later, they walked hand-in-hand through the entrance to the park. It was a bigger area than the local park in Torey Hope, but Zach knew Zoey could take what she saw and make it her own back in Torey Hope. He had no doubt she'd want to start the same type program.

When she saw the sign stating, "Yoga in the Park" she cocked her head and smiled at him.

"Are we doing yoga in the park?"

He had worn his own workout clothes, knowing he'd want to participate as well.

"Yep. And if you like the concept..." He trailed off, trying to see if she thought the idea sounded like something she'd want to do.

"We could do this in Torey Hope!"

She glanced back at the sign. "It's open to anyone to join for free. What an awesome way to give back to the community and teach them some beneficial techniques. I love it! Can we talk to Decker about getting it set up?"

He loved that he knew her well enough to know she would love this idea.

"I already mentioned it to Decker, he thinks it sounds like a great idea. We figure some people will only take advantage of the free park classes, but it's a good bet that many will like the yoga practice so well they'll come to The Center+ to get a more formal class. It's a win-win."

Zoey rubbed her hands together and smiled. "This is great. Not only do I get to spend a fabulous morning enjoying nature and yoga with my favorite guy, I also have a great idea to take back to Torey Hope. I love it, Zach. Thank you."

Her arms wrapped around his neck, pulling his lips down to meet hers. "This is *almost* as good as our hotel activities. Almost." She winked at him.

As they unrolled their borrowed mats, neither caught sight of the man hiding in the shadowy grove of trees. But, he saw them, and his blood boiled as he watched her in the arms of another.

"I DIDN'T REALIZE that doing yoga outside would make it even more invigorating. That was awesome, Zach, thanks so much for taking me. I know we have one more night here, but I'm chomping at the bit to get back to Torey Hope and get this all set up."

She talked a mile-a-minute over her turkey and cheese deli sandwich, and Zach couldn't help but smile. He loved that he had helped bring her the excitement, and he loved more that he had been there to experience it with her.

"What are you smiling at?" She tossed a chip at him. "I know I'm talking a lot, I'm just excited." A blush lit her face.

"I'm not judging with my smile, I'm just happy. Happy that you're so excited, happy I had a part to play in it, and happy I got to be here to experience it with you."

He checked his watch.

"We have to be at our final destination in two hours. Let's go change our clothes and maybe walk the town a bit. We can check out where we want to have supper tonight." He reached for the check, but her hand stopped him.

Looking up, he met her gaze.

"What's wrong, Zoey?"

Worrying her lip between her teeth, she huffed out a sigh. "I don't know, Zach, it's hard to explain."

"Try. You know I'll always listen to anything you have to say, even if it's hard to say or harder to understand." He rubbed her hand with a soft thumb.

"Sometimes, like now, when you're taking me to all these

great things, buying breakfast, buying lunch, treating me...I don't know, it's like I'm not capable of taking care of myself, or coming up with great ideas by myself." She frowned as she continued thinking through her thoughts.

"I've always been reliant on you. I'm the hometown girl, the one who graduated early just to stick around and wait for her dream to come home. Do you think that makes me look weak?" She raised serious eyes to him.

"Zoey, I think you are the strongest, most creative, smartest girl I know. I don't ever want to make you feel like you're trapped with me in Torey Hope. My dream has always been to settle in our hometown with you by my side, building The Center+, and making a life for ourselves. But, if you need more than that, I won't hold you back." He brushed her hair behind her ear. "Is this all about me paying for lunch?"

She smiled slightly, "No, that was just the catalyst for all the thoughts in my mind. I have the same dream as you, Zach. Ever since I was little, I've wanted to be part of the family business, and be by your side as we build it up. I'm out of high school, working towards my degree, working with you, helping with The Center+. I guess I just feel like everyone else has left for bigger things before coming back to settle down, but I've never really been anywhere. I don't want to leave forever, I just want to say I've been places."

She took a deep breath and let it out shakily.

"Does that even make sense?"

"Yeah, it does. And it's an easy fix. You and I will travel.

Once we get things settled a little more at The Center+ and you can work around your semester schedules, we will pick our top five places and start making plans to travel. Sound good?"

He knew deep down that his offered solution wasn't exactly what she was needing. His heart hurt at the thought of her wanting to be more independent because that meant he'd have to let her go, even if just for a while. But, until that day came, he'd be happy to travel the world with her.

She leaned in to kiss him. "Sounds wonderful. Let's start our lists soon. I'm feeling a bit anxious, like a bird ready to stretch its wings and fly."

Please, just don't stretch those wings and fly too far away from me, Zoey. I don't know if I could survive losing you. But if being away from me is what you need, I'll die a thousand deaths before I deny you what you need.

"I FEEL a little odd walking around in my gardening clothes, Zach."

She smiled up at him, her reddish-blonde hair shining in the sun from under her big floppy garden hat. She was shorter than him, but the cute little shorts she wore with her bright pink gardening boots made her legs look like they went on for miles.

"Well, you need to have on your gardening clothes so you

don't get dirty. And that's all you're getting out of me." He tapped her nose, and pointed to the quaint little diner across the street. "That's where we should eat dinner. Greasy cheeseburger, hot, salty fries, and a milkshake. Sounds good, right?"

"As someone who does yoga, strives to be a physical trainer, and likes to grow organic foods in my garden, I *should* be appalled at the artery-clogging foods you just listed. However, they sound so delicious, I can't help but agree with you. That's where we will eat dinner, but we have to go for a run afterwards." She cocked her head to see if he was up for it.

"If it means I get to eat that meal, I'll run." They both laughed and headed down the street into a more residential area.

Zach looked at his phone in confusion when a text came through.

"What's wrong? Who is it?" Zoey asked.

"Nothing's wrong. It's Kendrick, but I think he texted the wrong person." Zach shrugged and put his phone back into his pocket as they continued down a shady sidewalk.

"Do we know someone here? Are we visiting?" Zoey's curiosity was never quiet.

"Well, we are going to someone's house, but it's a friend of a friend, and we aren't exactly visiting, we are here to learn. Well, *you're* here to learn, and I'm here to learn how to assist." He knew his words would aggravate her even more.

"Stop talking in riddles!"

They arrived at a beautiful old home. Walking toward the back door, Zach turned to look at Zoey. "You coming?"

"Isn't it rude to go to a stranger's back door?"

"When I talked to her on the phone she said to come straight to the back door." He held out his hand for her.

She shrugged and walked with him.

They came to a back patio covered with lush flowering plants and surrounded with huge, well-maintained ferns and potted plants. Zoey immediately fell in love with this little oasis.

"When I have my own house, I want an area just like this." She closed her eyes and lifted her face to the plants as if to breathe in their beauty.

A woman about their grandmas' age came out the back door.

"Hi, I'm Ann. You must be Zach and Zoey." She reached a hand out to shake.

"Hi, I'm Zoey, you have a gorgeous home, but I think I could survive right here on your patio for the rest of my life. It's amazing."

"Thank you. We love it here. There's nothing I love more than sipping my coffee out here in the mornings, or watching my grandchildren play among the flowers." Ann pulled a couple chairs out and indicated they should sit.

"So, on the phone, Zach told me he had talked to a friend of a friend and heard about my garden. I saved a little bit of work so you could help me with it if you're up for that. And I'll show you the books and explain how I got everything set up." Ann spoke, but then looked around the patio. "Would you like to see the plants down here first? We can head up the hill to the garden in a bit."

"I'd love to see the plants down here and your garden." Zoey smiled at Ann, but looked curiously at Zach.

He shook his head and blushed a bit. "Sorry, I had kept this all a surprise from her, so I didn't tell her anything about your garden."

Turning to Zoey he spoke, "Ann has what's called a lasagna garden. When my friend told me about it, I knew it was right up your alley. So I called Ann to see if she'd teach you about it."

"You had me at 'garden', so let's get started." Zoey smiled at both Ann and Zach and took his hand as they toured the older woman's patio.

Zoey quickly pulled out her phone and began taking pictures and making notes about the types of plants Ann had growing.

Their tour was interspersed with Zoey's "ooohhhs" and "aahhhs" and the occasional "I've *got* to plant some of this!"

"Whew, it's starting to really warm up. I've got some cucumber, lemon, mint ice water if you're interested?" Ann offered the beverage, but then quickly added, "Or, I've got regular bottled water in the garage refrigerator."

She spoke with a smile which indicated she knew her water concoction maybe wasn't made for everyone.

"No, the water you described sounds delicious. I'll take a glass, please and thank you." Zoey spoke politely and looked at Zach.

"I'm always up for something new, I'll try it too." He shrugged good-naturedly.

As Ann walked through the back door to get their waters, Zoey turned to him and smiled from ear-to-ear.

"Oh my gosh, Zach! This is so amazing. Even if we just came to see her patio and drink her water, it would be worth it. But I've caught a few glimpses up the hill and her garden looks unbelievable! Thank you."

She leaned in and kissed him.

The three of them enjoyed the refreshing iced water in the shade of the patio.

"So, before we head up the hill, let me tell you a bit about lasagna gardening." Ann seemed to recognize she'd found a kindred spirit in her love of gardening with Zoey.

"Lasagna gardening is an easy no-dig, no-till organic gardening method that results in rich, fertile soil. The name 'lasagna gardening' has nothing to do with what you grow in the garden. It refers to the method of building the garden, which essentially is adding layers of organic materials that will 'cook down' over time, and provide rich soil for your plants. This method is great for the environment, because you're using your yard and kitchen waste and essentially composting it in place to make a new garden." Ann spoke knowledgeably and with enthusiasm.

"I'm sold already! Can we see your garden now?" Zoey was practically bouncing on her chair.

"Let's go." Ann placed the three empty glasses on a small cart and started up the hill toward her garden.

Over two hours later, sweaty, dirty, and happy, the three of them returned to the patio.

"Let me get everyone another glass of water." Ann quickly disappeared into her home, returning a few moments later with freshly poured glasses of iced water.

Zach had to admit, it was one of the most refreshing drinks he'd ever tasted.

"Ann, I can't thank you enough for showing me everything here today. Your patio and garden are amazing. I have enough pictures and notes to keep me busy for the next several months."

Zoey smiled excitedly and elbowed Zach in the stomach. "And this guy has the job of building me some raised garden beds so I can get started right away."

ONCE THEY WERE BACK at the hotel, the exhaustion from the day set in.

"Let's shower off the garden grime and take a nap." Zach made the suggestion knowing Zoey was tired, and because he wanted them to be able to enjoy the last night of their weekend without being worn out. Plus, he had every intention of wearing her out in other ways.

"Sounds like a great idea." She walked to the shower and turned in on. Walking back to stand by the bed, she slowly stripped her sweaty clothes from her body.

Turning on her heel and heading to the shower, she glanced over her shoulder with a grin, "I may need some help, if you know of anyone interested."

He swore she purposely swayed her bottom more than usual as she walked away from him. Groaning deep in his chest, he quickly removed his clothing and all but ran to the bathroom.

Climbing in the shower behind her, he gathered her in his arms.

"I think I may be able to be of assistance." He gruffly whispered in her ear.

Giggling, she turned in his arms, "Oh, good, I'm glad it's you. I don't let just anyone help me with my showers."

Kissing him, she laughed when he growled.

"Damn straight no one else is helping with your showers."

Several steamy minutes later, right as the water began to run cold, they climbed from the shower and stumbled to bed. For two hours, they slept cocooned in their blissful, exhausted state.

10

"Well, well, well, what are the chances of seeing you two here? Is it a family reunion? A kissing cousins convention?" The smarmy voice from behind him crawled up his neck and made him want to come out swinging.

Turning around, gripping Zoey tighter to his side, he faced the jackass who had spoken.

He didn't automatically recognize him, but he felt Zoey stiffen in his arms.

"Hi, Jason. What are you doing over here?" Zach noticed that she didn't acknowledge the douche bag's reference to them being cousins.

"Oh, just came over to get a taste of something bigger and better than Torey Hope. You know I'm not really cut out for the small town life. As soon as I'm done with school, I'm out of there. In fact, I'm already taking extra classes at the local college so I can get my degree quicker."

He looked at Zach with a sneer. "I'm going to be a chiropractor, making tons of cash, and I'll need a physical trainer on my team. Zoey and I have talked about partnering up and starting a practice."

"No, Jason, YOU talked about doing that. I told you I was quite happy with my work at The Center+. And after the weekend Zach and I have had, I've got even more plans for programs at work, so I definitely have no reason to leave The Center+ or Torey Hope." She gripped Zach's hand in hers.

"Do the good folk of Torey Hope know the esteemed sales manager at The Center+ is seducing under aged girls? I wonder how the town would feel to know a name they trust is getting down and dirty with a young, impressionable girl, especially a cousin." Jason's lip curled as he made his threatening remarks.

"Listen fuck head..." Zach started.

"I got this, Zach." Zoey kissed his cheek, and then turned her fire towards Jason.

"Listen, Jason. I told you a long time ago that you and I could be friends, but that was it. You've known for several years that I love Zach and that we aren't blood related. In regards to your slimy little threat, we are 100% within the law and statutes in the state of Illinois. The legal age of consent is 17 and that's the age I happen to be. So, you need to take your ridiculous threats and move on. Enjoy your break from the small town life; too bad you'll always be the small minded type."

She turned away quickly, grabbing Zach's hand, and led him into the diner where they'd stopped for dinner.

Zach couldn't resist turning around and flipping Jason the bird before laughing and following his favorite girl into the restaurant.

"Oh! The nerve of that asshole! I'm sorry if I went off a little too much. I just get so angry when a guy can't take no for an answer. He's been bugging me about going out with him since junior high. Once I finally got him to believe I didn't want to date him, he started in on the 'kissing cousins' thing. I even went so far as to show him a family tree to prove we aren't related. So, I guess now he's going to focus on the age thing." She threw the menu down, and growled.

"Hey, pretty girl. First, you were great out there. Second, settle down, don't let that prick get you so upset. Third, we know we've done nothing wrong. So even if he were to go tell the whole town, we'd know we are within the law and he doesn't have a leg to stand on. Plus, we come from families who are the cornerstone of Torey Hope. Jason and his family are wannabes. I'm glad to hear he's going to leave town soon." He reached over and smoothed her hair behind her ear.

"Ready for a big, greasy cheeseburger?"

She laughed, obviously trying to let go of her anger.

"Yes, with fries and a milkshake. I'm not going to let him ruin our last night here." She looked at the menu briefly and smiled broadly when the waitress came to take their order.

"So, I know this whole weekend has been a surprise for me, but I think I have a surprise for you too." She blushed and glanced at him shyly.

"Really? What's your surprise?" Zach couldn't imagine what she could have to surprise him with, but he was anxious to find out if it made her turn such a gorgeous shade of pink.

"Um, wow, this is sort of embarrassing. Actually, maybe I shouldn't tell you, I don't want you to be mad at me." She worried that pretty lip between her teeth.

"Oh no you don't. You can't blush and bring up a surprise and then go back on it. I'd never be mad at you. What did you do?" Zach captured her around the waist and pressed her against the wall.

"Well, I may have asked Kendrick..." She started.

"Oh, hell. This should be good." He laughed and kissed her neck.

"I may have asked Kendrick for ideas of things we could do without going all the way." She looked at him with worry.

"And?" Zach could only imagine what his crazy cousin had suggested.

"Well, I didn't have time to look at the bag he gave me. I just stuffed it in my bag and brought it along. I thought maybe we could take a look at what he sent."

Zach threw his head back, laughing.

When Zoey looked at him like he was crazy, he just shook his head.

"Remember that text I got from Kendrick earlier and I said I thought he had texted the wrong person? Well, all it said was 'You're welcome.' I didn't get it at the time, but I do now."

They both laughed.

After they each took quick, separate, showers, they piled onto the bed with the bag of goodies from Kendrick.

Sitting cross-legged, observing the bag hesitantly, they laughed nervously.

"Well, let's see what Kendrick has packed for us. Honestly, I'm a little frightened." Zach winked at her, and reached an arm slowly into the bag.

Pulling out a piece of paper, Zach unfolded a note. It was written in two separate scripts, so he knew two people had written on it. He laid it on the bed so they could both see it.

Scanning the paper, it was evident that Kendrick had written the first three-fourths of the letter, but Sawyer had added something at the very end.

They each took a deep breath and began to read the portion from Kendrick.

Well, well, well, my little cousin Zoey Belle has grown up so fast. One day she's asking me to cook her hotdog over the campfire, the next day she's asking me for things she can do with Zach's hotdog. They grow up so fast.

I asked Decker and Sawyer to help me with this project. Decker shook his head and declined. Sawyer pretty much refused, although he did throw in one item I think Zach may be extremely interested in.

I've labeled each item with title and use. If the item isn't in its original package, don't worry, it's been cleaned and sanitized. Kidding, kidding....mostly.

At this point, Zoey and Zach nearly choked on their laughter.

"Oh my God, did he pack USED items?!" Zoey was incredulous.

"We're talking about Kendrick, depravity and debauchery have his picture next to them in the dictionary." Zach shook his head at the ridiculousness of his cousin.

But, he knew Kendrick meant no harm. He probably knew they wouldn't use any of the items. They turned back to the letter.

So, I've included a variety of toys. Some meant for Zoey and some meant for Zach. Some are a little more tame, while some much more outlandish. Yes, I've used almost all of these at some point. You'll have to guess which is my favorite. Let me know which you like best, or find most intriguing, and I'll get it for you as an engagement gift.

They continued laughing, but both were putting off opening the bag out of sheer fear and embarrassment.

"Maybe we should just leave the bag closed?" Zoey suggested.

"No way, now we have to follow this through. He probably thinks we won't open the bag, or we'll be intimidated. We've got to at least go through the bag, and maybe try out something tame so he doesn't get one over on us."

They resumed reading the letter, finding a brief sentence from Sawyer.

So, I don't have a lot of experience with sex toys for girls, but I DO have some expertise in what guys like. So, I included a brand-new, unopened, unused item I think Zach will find extremely useful. Enjoy, Cuz!

Zoey looked intrigued, Zach felt his stomach plummet as he wondered just what a homosexual man would consider a good sex toy for him and Zoey to use.

"Okay, let's get this show on the road." Zach nodded to Zoey to indicate she should pick something from the bag.

Adopting her best Vanna White, television announcer persona, Zoey pulled out a cardboard box. Reading the sticky note, she said aloud:

This is a pocket rocket. It's brand new. If you do nothing with the rest of what I've lovingly packaged here, please consider using this.

Zoey bit her lip as she looked at the box. It was just plain cardboard. Zach could tell she was curious, so he nodded at her.

Blushing, she opened the box and removed the device. Palming it in her hand, she looked it over.

Watching her study the inconspicuous toy made Zach very aware of certain parts of his anatomy. How he would get through her inspecting more outrageous items, he had no clue. Kendrick was going to pay for this.

"Well, I think we can keep this one on the 'maybe' list." She smiled shyly, reached into the bag again.

"He's packed them sort of in an order, so I'm just going to go through what comes next."

Zoey pulled the next item out, and began to read.

This is a butterfly. It's awesome, but it may make Zach look bad if you use it before you use him. So maybe save it for later. You can have this one, it's only been used once.

Zoey squealed as she dropped the toy.

"Eeww, I don't care if he boiled it, there's no way I'm using that."

Zach chuckled, "I'm pretty sure Kendrick knows we won't be using most of this stuff. He's just giving us both a hard time."

Nipple clamps, and a coil of cotton rope and blindfold came next. Zoey dumped the nipple clamps with the butterfly. She studied the rope and blindfold. Placing them gently to the side, but not with the 'no way' items, she blushed.

"Maybe one day. Not now, but I'm not saying never."

Zach knew he was going to make a mess of his shorts before the night was over.

A pair of edible panties and whipped cream came next. The panties joined the 'one day' pile. The whipped cream won a spot in the 'maybe' pile.

She hesitantly inspected the next item and read the note.

This is a butt plug. Likely way too advanced for you. But, the girl who wanted me to use this on her really liked it.

The butt plug zinged through the air as Zoey hurled it against the wall.

"Kendrick Robert Jordan! You better HOPE you didn't really pack a used butt plug in that bag!" She yelled to no one in particular but laughed as she did it.

Leaning across the bag to kiss her, Zach laughed too. "I want to say he'd never really do that, but I can't say it with 100% certainty. We all know how Kendrick is."

Pulling the last item from the bag, they realized it was the addition from Sawyer. Zach's mouth dropped open as Zoey read the sticky note penned in Sawyer's script.

This is a prostate stimulator. Zach, I'm assuming you've never had a prostate orgasm. Use the lube included in the box, let Zoey do the work. You just lie back and enjoy. You're welcome.

Expecting the toy to immediately go in the 'no way' pile, Zach's eyebrows raised a good three inches when she bit her lip and confidently tossed the box into the pile with the vibrator and whipped cream.

Holy shit.

"So, pretty girl, you really want to use *all* those things?" His voice sounded hesitant.

Biting her lip, Zoey nodded slowly. The little imp.

"It's only three items. And it seems like we can share in the fun. After all, I don't want this to be only about me."

Thinking maybe he could distract her, Zach pushed the items from the bed and rolled her under him. Kissing her thoroughly, he felt the shivers in her body as his hands traveled up her torso.

"Just making sure there's no miscommunication here, Zo. We can play around, but no actual sex tonight." He spoke gruffly, part of him wanting badly to throw his morals out the proverbial window, but he let his tongue trace her neck, making goosebumps appear along her skin.

"We're on the same page. But I very much want to use those toys if you're game."

Grabbing the vibrator and whipped cream, he placed them on the bedside table.

"In due time. Patience is a virtue and all that." He smiled smugly at her.

After a sensual stripping of her clothes, he removed most of his, leaving his boxer briefs on in hopes of containing his raging desire. And also in hopes of protecting his *virtue* from the toy Sawyer had packed.

"Mmmm, I'm thinking a Zoey sundae sounds pretty tasty right about now." He laughed and licked his lips in a cartoonish way.

When he'd applied the whipped cream to all of her most delicious parts, he began to systematically remove each dollop with his lips and tongue.

When his tongue reached her very center, he reached for the vibrator and paused long enough to look askance up at her from his position.

Nodding her head in assent, he tore the box open.

Several moments later, Zoey whimpered as he moved up her body to lick the last of the sticky whipped cream from her mouth.

"You're beautiful when you let go like that, pretty girl. I can't wait to see it happen when it's me instead of that pink rubber toy."

She giggled, completely sated.

"I'm going to pay Kendrick back by describing, in great detail, how much I love that vibrator. In fact, I'm going to really play it up regarding *all* the toys."

Zach threw his head back and laughed.

"Yeah, that would serve him right. The more details, the better."

Zoey rolled over and ran her nails down his chest.

"I think I'm still in the mood for something sweet.

Where's that whipped cream?"

Losing the battle to keep his boxers on, he lifted up slightly so she could get to what she was seeking.

After applying the whipped cream, Zoey sat back on her heels and admired her work.

"It's so pretty, I almost hate to eat it." Her voice held a teasing tone.

"You don't have to do anything you don't want to, Zo." His voice was strained, but he didn't want her to feel forced.

"I didn't say I didn't *want* to." She spoke softly as she lowered her mouth to the mound of whipped cream.

Going slowly, she experimented with different things, and he was sure to let her know what felt best. When he was within moments of it all being over, she stopped and looked up at him seductively.

"I really want to try that thing Sawyer sent."

Oh, hell.

"I don't know, Zoey, that's not really something I've ever had a desire to try." His voice was laced with equal parts hesitation and desire. He knew with little prodding she could talk him into just about anything at the moment.

"Let's just see what happens. Just like you promised to stop at any time, I'll do the same. But, there's got to be something to it, or you wouldn't see all these gay guys loving anal sex. If it was all terrible, they'd stop doing it. So the magical prostate has to be worth something." She reached down to grab the box. "Besides, it's not like I'm asking you to have actual anal sex, but Sawyer promises this will be awesome."

She stopped talking, holding the toy in her hand along with a small bottle of lube. Looking at him expectantly, he gave up and nodded his agreement.

She popped open the lube and poured it in her hand.

Grasping him in her fist, she moved slowly up and down.

"Zoey, not that I'm complaining here. Not at all. But, you seem to have quite a bit of knowledge, if not hands-on practice, about some things. You been talking to people, pretty girl?"

She blushed. Pouring more lube on the toy, her hand, and dribbling the cool liquid on his ass while he gasped in surprise, she hesitated.

"Um, I may have talked a little to Luke about hand jobs and blow jobs. And I have read enough male/male romance books to know the basics of anal sex."

Fighting off the desire barreling through his body, Zach grabbed hold and clung to the feeling of surprise that last statement gave him, while he spread his legs for her with very little thought as to what he was doing.

"You're reading male/male romance books?"

Shrugging her shoulders nonchalantly as she continued her left-handed assault on his erection, and began her right-handed exploration of his ass, she quipped, "Sure. It's hot. I got interested in the genre when Sawyer left a book laying out on the coffee table. I was intrigued, and now I'm sort of hooked."

All talking ceased when she let her fingers brush against an area no one had ever been that close to, unless one counted the doctors making him turn his head and cough for sports physicals.

"I'm going to do this really slowly. Don't clench up. This is fairly small, and very slick, but it may burn a bit. It might help if you push out against it as it goes in."

As she ever-so-slowly advanced the toy into never-never land, he almost stopped breathing when she took his length back into her hands.

Reaching up, he grasped his base. He didn't want to end things just as they were starting to get interesting. He'd come this far, might as well see it through. Right?

Wrong! Dear God, the burn as the head of the toy breached the ring of muscles he'd never thought would be breached in that way was breathtaking. And not in a good way.

Zoey grimaced when his breath caught. "I know it burns. Well, I'd imagine it burns. Give it just a moment. If it's still terrible, we'll stop."

Zoey moved the stimulator fractionally, and turned on the vibrations.

He thought he'd fly off the bed. Arching his back, he felt shots of electricity fire through every nerve-ending of his body. Yep, she'd found what she was looking for.

"Do you want me to stop?" Zoey hesitated.

"No!"

His body took flight. The sensation was so much more than he'd ever experienced. The relentless vibrations against that newly discovered bundle of nerves, her hand stroking his length, his entire body was electrified, like his veins were filled with molten electric currents.

When he came back to earth, he opened his eyes and brought his earth-angel into focus. She was looking at him expectantly.

"So? Was it okay? Worth it?" She looked scared he was going to say it was horrible.

Completely sated, like he was floating on warm clouds and could sleep for a week, he let his eyes flutter shut as he spoke.

"Let's just say, I now completely get why some people enjoy anal sex. And Sawyer and Luke are *damn* lucky."

After a quick tissue wipe down, he pulled her close to his chest, turning them both so he could spoon her.

"We will definitely be keeping that particular gift." His voice whispered against her ear.

They both giggled and fell into a completely satisfied sleep.

11

*Z*ach and Zoey were back at work the next day. After avoiding the smirky smiles of Kendrick all day, Zoey texted all her cousins.

Zoey: Feel like we haven't been out together for a while. Want to meet up for dinner tonight?

A few moments later her phone was abuzz with activity.

Decker: Sure. Kate and I will be there. 7:00? Usual place?

Sawyer: I'll check with Luke, but I'm pretty sure we can both make it. See you then.

Kendrick: Wouldn't miss it.

Aly: I'll try to make it.

Zach walked into the studio to find Zoey stretching for her next class. He chuckled as he read Kendrick's reply.

"Poor guy. Probably thinks he's going to get to embarrass us. Little does he know your descriptive retelling is waiting for him."

He pulled her to her feet and wrapped his arms around her waist. Leaning down to kiss her lightly, he fought the urge to gather her up and escape work just to spend the day kissing her.

Groaning, he broke the kiss. "Sorry, just needed a moment. I'll drive us to dinner. Pick you up at 6:45?"

Smacking one last kiss against his lips, Zoey grinned up at him, "I'll be ready."

"YOUR TABLE IS READY, follow me please." The hostess at the neighborhood grill and sports bar gathered the menus and led them to their table.

Once seats were situated, drinks and meals ordered, the real chit-chat began.

Decker, not usually one to joke around a lot, leaned back in his chair with his arm around Kate. His eyes shone with humor. Zach, and everyone at the table, could see how good Kate was for Decker. He'd opened up, loosened up, and seemed to actually take time for fun these days.

With his laughing eyes, Decker spoke. "So, I let you two take a few days off. How'd that go?"

He fought back his laughter, attempting to keep the question professional, but everyone around the table knew he was referring to more than just the outside-the-bedroom activities from the weekend.

Snorts sounded around the table, but Zoey and Zach chose to ignore them. Zach knew Zoey was a bit hurt and pissed that Aly hadn't shown up, but also knew she was determined to enjoy their evening, and eventually get a chance to put Kendrick in his place.

"Thanks for asking, Deck. The trip was great." She rolled her eyes, and continued on as if nothing had happened when Kendrick snorted again.

"I've got a great plan for a yoga program. It will involve free yoga classes in the park, along with increased yoga classes at The Center+. On a personal level," she paused, appearing to gather her thoughts, but really she was just stringing Kendrick along.

Zach played along, grabbing her hand and whispering loudly enough for the whole table to hear. "Baby, you don't have to talk about the personal stuff."

"No, Zach, I want to share. It was so awesome, I want to tell everyone about it."

Luke and Sawyer cast wide-eyed, unbelieving looks at each other. Katie's mouth dropped into a little O as she reached for Decker's hand. Kendrick leaned back in his chair, smugly crossing his arms across his chest.

"Yeah, Zach, let her tell us about the personal stuff."

Taking a deep breath, she sighed dramatically.

"Oh, Kendrick, it was so amazing. First, we saw these gorgeous tropical plants and hundreds of butterflies. I can't grow the tropical plants all that well in our temperate climate, but I'm definitely planting a butterfly bush in my garden to attract more butterflies. They are so fragile, and beautiful, and peaceful. Speaking of gardens, I've got about a gazillion plans on making a new garden. It's called 'lasagna gardening', and Zach's going to help me get it all built and set up. I think it will be so much easier, and healthier, and good for the environment. I'm so excited. The weekend was definitely satisfying."

She stopped and looked around the table. There was a long pause, like everyone was waiting to see if she was joking or if there was more she was going to tell.

"Ohhhh, wait. Kendrick, you were wanting to know about the sexual stuff, right?" Zoey spoke a bit louder than most at the table were comfortable with.

"Uh-oh, I don't think this is going to go well." Luke whispered to Sawyer.

"Well, let me tell you. We both *greatly* appreciated your bag of goodies, didn't we?" She glanced at Zach who was fighting to keep his face from busting into laughter.

"Yep, *greatly*."

He knew her plan was talk in great, raunchy detail about all the items they *didn't* use, in hopes of giving Kendrick some of his own medicine.

"Well, the blind fold was a great addition. I think the burns from the rope are almost gone." She dramatically looked at her wrists. Luckily it was dark enough the others couldn't tell there weren't really any burns.

"We used a little rubbing alcohol on the butterfly and butt plug, just to make sure they were sanitized from their last use." Zoey spoke across the table, never taking her eyes from Kendrick's. Zach knew if she looked at any of the others she would mess it up and start laughing.

"So, yeah, nipple clamps. Who knew? Mine are pretty small so I was afraid they wouldn't work, but whoa baby! Major turn on. I think I came once just from Zach tugging on those." She shook her head as if trying to clear the memory.

Kendrick's face was pale.

"And the butterfly? Man, talk about perfect clit stimulation. And once we got the butt plug in correctly, the third orgasm was the most intense I've ever had."

Kendrick's face had started to scrunch up, like he'd seen something disgusting.

"And, I can't speak for the flavor of the edible panties, but

Zach sure seemed to enjoy feasting on them. And I know I definitely wasn't complaining when he got past the panties and started in on me."

Kendrick looked like he was going to puke.

"For the love of all that's holy, please just stop." He held his hands to his ears.

Looking as innocent as possible, Zoey stood and looked at Katie. "I need to pee, want to go with me?"

Katie, shocked and mute, just nodded and stood.

As they began to leave the table, Zoey turned on her heel and walked back a few feet.

Standing directly behind Kendrick, she bent down to his ear. "Everything I just said was a complete and total lie, invented to get you back for being a depraved and raunchy human being. None of that happened. You sent us *used* sex toys, Kendrick? You are so wrong, on so many levels. But we love you. Just always remember that payback is a bitch."

She smiled sweetly at him as she walked away. Zach cracked up laughing.

"Man, you should have *seen* your face! Priceless!"

Once in the bathroom, Katie and Zoey were practically on the floor rolling.

"That was so awesome. I kept sitting there trying to gauge your face to see if you were serious, but you held it together so well. I was in total shock at what you were telling the whole table, but then I thought, *Well, good for her.* I wish we'd caught his face on video." Katie had to wipe tears from her eyes as she spoke.

Once back at the table, Zoey announced that she and Katie were going to go check on Aly. They left the boys to do their boy stuff.

Kendrick watched the door close behind them, then turned to the waitress and ordered everyone another beer.

"Okay, so maybe I went a bit overboard with the toys. But did you at least use some of them?" His curiosity was killing him, Zach could see that much.

"I'm not going to give you sexual details on my weekend with your *cousin*. We may or may not have used some of the items, but it's none of your business. Man, maybe you need to go find one of your hundreds of willing girls and get laid. You're entirely too interested in my sex life."

"Whoa, wait, sex life? As in you guys had sex? I thought you wanted to wait until her birthday." Decker seemed concerned.

"No, that's still the plan. I won't mess that up. I just meant sex life in regards to everything else we may or may not have done, using or not using the 'bag of depravity' Kendrick sent along in hopes of shocking us." Zach swigged his beer, shaking his head in memory of the bag o'toys.

"I do have one question. Were those really *used* toys?" Zach squinted his eyes in hopes of reading his cousin's face.

Much of his smugness gone, Kendrick pouted a bit.

"If you're not sharing info, neither am I. I just say you

should think about the type of person I am, and ask yourself if I'd really send you used sex toys."

The entire table cracked up at his answer.

"Okay, now that the girls are gone, I've got to ask." Sawyer leaned in closer.

Zach was glad they'd been seated in the back of the restaurant where no one else was sitting. He knew what was coming. He busied himself with the label on his beer, willing himself not to blush.

To his right, Luke was trying his best not to laugh.

To his left, Decker was shaking his head.

Straight ahead, Kendrick looked truly intrigued.

And Sawyer had a look on his face that said, "If you did what I think you did, all I can say is I told you so."

"So, what do you have to ask?" Zach decided he'd try to play dumb for a bit. Maybe they'd get distracted.

"Man, you don't even have to answer. I don't even know what the question is, but we can all see from the look on your face that the answer is *yes*." Decker smirked at him.

Zach shook his head, trying his best not to blush, and glanced toward Sawyer and Luke.

"I'll say this. If *that* happens every time, I have a brand new outlook on what the two of you are doing behind closed doors."

When everyone had gathered themselves from the fit of laughter, Kendrick leaned back, hands behind his head.

"So, that good huh?" The gears in his head were obliviously grinding.

Zach just nodded. But Luke and Sawyer bobbed their heads enthusiastically.

"I'm going to need to try that. Real dick, finger, or toy? Which is better?" He asked in complete seriousness.

"There are times I sit back and listen to you talk and wonder how the hell we've all stayed friends over the years." Decker just laughed good-naturedly, and swigged his beer while he listened to the answer.

"I'll bow out of this one due to lack of experience." Zach sat back from the table.

"Well, I'm going to have to go with real dick or finger, but I don't have any positive experience with inanimate objects up my ass, so I can't speak in that area." Luke let Sawyer take his hand as a flash of pain clouded his eyes.

"So, I guess that leaves me as the resident expert." Sawyer chuckled. "Yeah, real dick is best. Because it's got a warm body attached to it, there's bound to be a lot of full body contact. Then a toy, because it can reach things better. A finger is fine in a pinch, but it can be hard to reach where it needs to reach, especially if there's not been a lot of practice."

Kendrick and Zach were both watching their cousin closely.

"What?" Sawyer asked.

"I'm just trying to wrap my head around the fact it could be any more intense." Zach shook his head incredulously.

"I'm just trying to think where I could get a real dick willing to take me home for the night and show me the world."

Kendrick replied with a completely straight face, but the guys all knew he was probably joking. Mostly. Somewhat. What the hell, one never knew when it came to Kendrick.

ZOEY AND KATIE rounded the back fence at the Morgan home. Zoey hesitated a bit, not wanting to interrupt Aly if she was busy. Instead, they found her lounging on a chaise, ear buds in, magazine in hand.

"What the hell, Aly? I thought you said you were busy tonight, and that's why you couldn't make dinner with the group?" Zoey tried to keep the hurt and irritation out of her voice.

Removing her ear buds and looking annoyed, Aly huffed, "No, I said I couldn't make it tonight. I didn't say I had plans or was busy, you just assumed that part."

"Semantics, Al! Why would you choose to sit at home by yourself when you know half of your family, the half that includes your best friend, is all out to dinner?"

"Oh, gee, let me think about that, Zoey. Maybe because Decker has Katie, Sawyer has Luke, Zach has you, did you ever think that maybe I didn't want to be the extra baggage on all the love trains?" Aly's words were heated, but her eyes held hurt.

Zoey stood still for a moment and watched as her best friend pretended to thumb through a magazine.

"Kendrick was by himself, coming single shouldn't have even crossed your mind. It was a family get together, Aly, not a group date." Exasperated, Zoey flung herself into a lounge chair.

Katie watched the exchange going on in front of her then spoke.

"Girls, I hate to see you two at odds like this. I know in the beginning it was an adjustment having the boys back in town. But we are several months removed from that."

Turning to Aly, Katie continued.

"Aly, you know part of why I'm good at my job is that I don't sugar coat things. You're being a brat right now. From what I've heard in stories, your nose got bent out of shape early on when Zoey and Zach started spending so much time together, and you've held onto that grudge and let it grow bigger and uglier over the years. Now that Zach's home for good, and he and Zoey are together and happy, you're letting it fester. I don't pretend to know why you're so mad, but I've got to tell you that life's too short to live angry. Embrace the fact that you have a fabulous family, great friends, and a bright future ahead of you." Katie perched on the edge of the chaise lounge, and pulled Aly into a hug.

Zoey hesitated momentarily, then joined in the hug.

"I love you, Aly. I just want us to all be happy. I want my friend back." Zoey whispered in her ear.

"I don't know why I'm so angry and upset about this. I promise I'll try harder. I miss being around all of you, I just don't want to be the third wheel or the one to bring everyone down." Aly sniffled as she spoke, fighting away the tears.

The girls spent the next hour laughing hysterically about the bag of sex toys, and the look on Kendrick's face as Zoey put him in his place.

Leaving Aly's house that night, Zoey felt like they were in a better place. For the time being.

12
_____

"Okay, so we're all set, right?" Zach talked to the guys in Decker's office at lunchtime.

"Yep, family birthday dinner at the Captain's house Thursday night. Cousins only party at our place on Friday night. Then Zoey is officially eighteen on Sunday." Kendrick wagged his eyebrows suggestively.

"What about Asher? Is he invited to the cousin party?" Zach questioned.

"Yeah, Josie and Kyle said he could come, but they want him to leave at 10:00pm. So that gives him time to hang out, feel like a big guy, then we can really turn loose after he leaves." Kendrick answered.

"If by 'really turn loose' you mean cuss a little more and maybe drink a little, that's fine. But we aren't throwing a sexed-up kegger for an eighteen year old's birthday party. No orgies, Kendrick." Decker's voice held a warning.

"A few more curse words, a little drinking, no orgying, got it." Kendrick winked at them all.

"Is 'orgying' even a word?" Sawyer asked.

"I just made it one. To orgy or not to orgy. We orgied in the past. We are orgying tonight. We will be orgying next week. I like it, it works for me." Kendrick waved as he left the office laughing.

"That man isn't right." Zach shook his head.

"No, no he's not." Decker agreed.

After a few moments in which all three men contemplated their cousin's antics, Sawyer cleared his throat and changed the subject.

"Okay, so what do we need to do for Friday night? Luke and I will make something for Thursday's dinner, but what's needed most for the cousin party?"

"Well, the Captain and Janie said to just bring whatever on Thursday. They will provide the main meal, but everyone else can bring sides or desserts. But, for Friday, I thought we'd do something easy like pizza. I guess it should be BYOB. Zach, as long as Zoey's staying at the house, I don't mind her drinking a little, but let's make sure it stays to a minimum." Decker spoke. Could you ever *really* change a control freak?

"I agree. I know she's had some alcohol before, but I don't want it going overboard. And I especially don't need Aly getting toasted; you think she's annoying sober, just wait until she's drunk."

"Luke and I will do a veggie and fruit tray." Sawyer was writing down a list so he could tell Luke what he'd volunteered them for.

Kendrick came back in whistling.

"Zach, you need to make those crispy rice treats. A triple batch. I don't know why yours are so much better, but you blow everyone else's out of the water."

Zach eyed his cousin to see if he was joking. When it was clear that he wasn't, Zach shrugged his shoulders and agreed to make the treats.

"Oh, I talked to Grandma Janie, she's doing cupcakes for the family party and a small cake for the cousin party." Decker read through his list.

"Wait, is any of this a surprise? Does Zoey know these plans?" Sawyer questioned.

"Do you actually think a surprise can be kept secret in this family?" Zach retorted.

"I don't know, Sawyer kept his 'I like cock' surprise secret for quite a while." Kendrick pointed out.

"Only one other person knew that secret, way too many people know this one. So I'm assuming it's *not* a surprise, right?" Sawyer laughed and rolled his eyes.

"Right, no surprise. Just bring what you're supposed to, when you're supposed to, and all will go fine." Decker nodded, and their impromptu lunchtime meeting ended.

~

ZACH LOOKED around the room at his entire family. Sometimes he had to stop and remind himself that his family situation was quite different than some. A family as large as the Morgan, Jordan, Martin clan was bound to have disagreements, and they'd had their share over the years. From the grandparents arguing with the parents, to the parents disagreeing with each other about the kids, to the kids having brawls during a backyard game of football, or the tiff that Aly and Zoey were having, all of those things happened and were normal. But, as he looked around at the love and laughter on each family member's face, and knew they were all here just to enjoy the company and wish Zoey a happy birthday, it made his heart warm and a smile come to his face. He wanted to keep the image in his mind, and never take his good fortune for granted.

"The food looks great, Captain and Janie." Kendrick gave his grandparents a hug, before moving on to his Grandparents Morgan and Grandparents Jordan.

Pausing to whisper loudly at Zach and Sawyer, he quipped, "Although, I'm pretty sure Zach's more in the mood for a certain taco, and Sawyer would rather be having hot dogs and buns."

"Lord, Kendrick, you really need to get new material

when it comes to your sexual innuendos with food, son." Audrey bopped him on the head and just shook her head.

They were missing a few people, but still needed to seat twenty-one bodies. As was usual over the years, the 'kids' gravitated toward one table and the 'grown ups' staked another. Laughter and good food was plentiful as it always was during their get togethers.

After the dinner dishes were done, Kendrick announced it was time for a game in the basement. Once everyone was gathered, he began the instructions.

"Okay, so life pretty much sucks and everything turns to shit."

Everyone seated around the large all-purpose room looked at Kendrick with wondering eyes. Jeremiah and Audrey Jordan observed their son curiously, a flash of worry darkening both of their faces.

"I mean, yeah, we've got it great in this family, but overall the world is a fucked up place. Bad people do bad things. Good people get screwed. It's all a part of life." Kendrick spouted his words in a very un-Kendrick-like way.

"Son, is this little motivational speech part of the game?" The Captain quirked an eyebrow.

Staring off into space momentarily, Kendrick appeared to gather himself.

Zach and Zoey, and most of the others in the room, gave each other looks that seemed to say *What the hell was that?*

Only Jeremiah and Audrey didn't seem confused, they just seemed concerned.

There was no time to dwell on the weirdness because Kendrick had started the game instructions.

"Okay, this is a combo of drawing and acting. You can draw your clues, or act out your clues, or combine the two. The only thing is no talking. *And* everything your team decides to draw/act has to be somehow related to the family. For example, a simple one would be drawing an Army uniform, a fishing pole, and acting like you were marching or saluting. Everyone would guess the answer is the Captain. You can go easy with answers being a person, or you can choose a phrase, or an event. Just write the type of clue on the paper when you begin so we can all see it. Points go to the teams who guess the clue, and the team playing the clue gets points if someone guesses correctly too. Okay, my team is me, Aly, and Asher, the rest of you losers are on your own. Team up!"

Zach smiled as he realized Kendrick had done what Kendrick did best. Taken the serious attention off himself, and helped out the two people in the room who were probably the most self-conscious of being alone. But, Zach was pretty sure Kendrick's little outburst hadn't been forgotten by most in the room.

The teams consisted of mostly couples, although there was a bit of switching. Decker and Sawyer teamed up, while Katie and Luke were a pair. Libby and Audrey started planning their clues immediately, which left Jeremiah and Nate to shrug their shoulders and be a team.

Over the next two hours, hilarity ensued as clue after clue was drawn and acted out.

The Captain and Janie got points when someone guessed "The Cakery".

Jack and Judy won their round when their word "grandchildren" was guessed.

John and Cindy earned points for drawing and acting out "love".

When it was Nicky and Carly's turn, Nicky whispered excitedly in her ear, and she just laughed. Nicky wrote "phrase" on the paper. Then he walked around with his stomach protruding, rubbing his back. Carly giggled, then helped him to the floor where he panted, and made the most awful faces.

Zach had heard all the stories about his dad being obsessed with Nate and Libby having babies in the past, way before he himself was born, so he figured it out pretty quickly. From the laughter floating around the circle of family, so did everyone else. But, because they all knew how much Nicky was enjoying himself, they let him play the clue out.

He pretended to wipe his brow, and breathed what appeared to be a sigh of relief. Then he graciously took the item Carly pretended to hand to him. He rocked it back and forth in his arms. When he started to lift his shirt to act out breastfeeding, Nate interrupted quickly.

"Whoa there, I think I've got it! Is it 'having a baby'?" Nate couldn't keep the grin from his face when he offered his answer.

Nicky nodded his head enthusiastically. "Yes! I knew you guys would get it right! It's what I used to always talk about."

Decker and Sawyer earned points, and plenty of groans from the group, when they drew clues for the phrase "Sawyer is gay."

By the last round, however, Kendrick's team with Asher and Aly had pretty much run away with the game.

"Okay, we could actually quit now, since my team is ahead, but I have one more clue for all you wonderful people." Kendrick wrote the word phrase on the paper and began drawing the clues while Aly and Asher acted them out.

In the end, it was clear that Decker, Sawyer, Katie, Luke, Zach, and Zoey all knew what the phrase was, but none of them would say it.

Zach took Zoey's hand, and leaned in to whisper in her ear. She nodded her head yes.

Zach looked around at the group, and realized quickly that *everyone* had figured out the phrase, but no one wanted to out the couple if it wasn't what they wanted.

"So, thanks Kendrick, for that awkward opening into telling everyone. I think." Zach darted slightly frustrated eyes at his cousin, and laughed a bit nervously.

"What? It's not like we don't all know you two are in love.

And this was as good as time as any to make it official." Kendrick nodded his head at the two.

"Okay, so the phrase Kendrick was getting at is *Zach and Zoey are dating*. I don't think this is really a surprise to most of you, you all know I've loved her since the very beginning. We just didn't want to make it weird on anyone if you see me kiss her or something." Zach took a deep breath and pulled Zoey close to his side.

It was a move he'd made a thousand times over the years, but it was different now. It meant the same, yet it meant something very different.

Smiles, nods of approval, and tears filled the room.

It wasn't as if Zach had expected resistance or disapproval, he just wasn't sure how the older generation would feel about watching them grow up together as friends, and then turn into something more.

"Starting out as friends is the best foundation you can build." Grandma Cindy hugged them both then scurried to get plates and napkins ready.

"You have a whole history together, and a whole future to create as well." Patting their cheeks, Grandma Judy headed to get the coffee started.

"Don't ever let anyone make you feel that what you have is wrong. Your love is beautiful, and true, and forever." Grandma Janie grasped their hands before going to plate the cupcakes.

"See, that went well. You're welcome." Kendrick stood behind them and pulled them both into a bear hug.

He was right, it had gone well. They hadn't been purposely hiding anything, they just hadn't made out in front of many family members yet, and they didn't want to shock anyone. Kendrick made it easy. But, it still felt a little strange to kiss her with all the grandpas sitting around.

Zach glanced around at the room, and saw that no one was paying any attention to them.

His heart warmed at how she instinctively curled into him when he put his arm around her shoulders.

When her face lifted to his with a smile, everyone else in the room disappeared.

"Whatcha thinkin', pretty girl?" He brushed a kiss against her lips.

"That I really want a cupcake." She giggled.

Throwing his head back in laughter, he tipped her chin up. "Is that *all* you're thinking about?"

"Mmm, cupcakes and my birthday. Specifically what we can do *after* my birthday." She let her lips touch his lightly as she spoke in a whisper.

"*After?* Oh, hell no. Saturday night, midnight."

They both laughed, knowing her birthday falling on Sunday wasn't the most convenient for what they had planned.

"In all seriousness, Zoey, Sunday isn't going to work out because of church and family stuff. You know we'll all be together most of the day. And I don't want anything to be rushed, so something during the week seems too forced. I'm definitely not asking your dad if we can go out of town again. The first time, he knew I was protecting your virtue and all that. This time, he's likely to castrate me before agreeing to me taking his little girl to a hotel room out of town."

Zach shuddered as he thought of it.

Laughing, Zoey nodded, "You're right. Let's just play it by ear and see what happens. We don't need a specific plan, it would feel too much like prom night."

"Whoa, what kind of plan did you have on your prom night?" Zach leaned back from her, pretending to be shocked.

Smacking him in the chest, she giggled, "Not *me*, you goof. I just heard a lot of my friends planning perfect prom night sex, and I always thought that nothing good was ever going to come from it. Too much planning, too many expectations, too much pressure."

They fell silent for a moment, just cuddling on the couch while they lovingly watched their family around them. All was good.

"Want to get that cupcake now?" Zach stood and reached his hand down to pull her up.

"Mmmm, yes." She licked her lips.

Zach wasn't sure if the move was meant to be seductive, but he had to adjust himself while walking up the stairs so his grandmothers wouldn't notice the bulge behind his zipper.

13

Opening the door to her car as she left work, Zoey could only smile as her eyes landed on the huge bouquet of flowers. Sliding a finger under the flap of the card, she felt her smile grow bigger.

To the most beautiful girl in the world. Happy birthday.

Taking the flowers in when she reached home, and laying the card on the table, Zoey all but bounded out the door when Zach pulled in about fifteen minutes later. Stopping to hug her parents, she spoke to them about the plans.

"We are having pizza, veggies, fruit, cake, and other goodies. Probably playing games or watching scary movies. Asher will be home a little after 10:00pm. Someone will bring him home. There will be some drinking going on while he's there, but only by those in the group who are legal. I plan on sleeping over at the guys' house, mainly because it appears that everyone else is. I may drink, but I won't drive, and the guys will keep me safe."

Josie and Kyle hugged her close. Each of them kissing her head.

Zach, sat in his truck for a few minutes and watched them. He knew from the look in their eyes, they were picturing her as a newborn baby, and probably wondering how she was turning eighteen in just a few days. It was clear they trusted Zoey, and knew she was more responsible than most, but he got the feeling that watching your child grow up and spread her wings was a very bittersweet emotion.

Zach climbed from the truck.

Shaking Kyle's hand, he smiled a bit.

"There may be some drinking, but we won't have a replay of the last time Zoey and Aly got hold of liquor. No worries, I'll guard her with my life. And Asher, too. We all love that kid, and feel like we missed out on some of his growing up years while we were in college. So, we like having him around. We'll be on our good behavior." Zach assured his pseudo aunt and uncle.

"Just your *good* behavior? I thought guys who wanted to take my daughter to their home for a party and sleepover would be promising *best* behavior." Kyle quirked a pierced eyebrow, and flicked the metal ring in his lip with his tongue.

If Zach didn't know the man, didn't know he was just

trying to give him a hard time, he'd be petrified of the tattoos, piercings, dyed hair, and tough guy persona. But, he knew that Kyle Martin marched to the beat of his own drummer and had a heart of gold. Not that he'd ever want to piss him off by screwing with his family, but he knew the man was just joking.

"Well, I can promise *good* behavior. I didn't go as far as saying *best* behavior, because we *are* talking about Kendrick in this equation. I make no promises where he's concerned." Zach just shook his head.

"Point made. Understood. You all have a good evening. We'll be here if you need anything. Probably having hot, kinky sex, so make sure it's important if you need to call." Kyle wagged his eyebrows.

Asher came in on the very end of the conversation, and had to cover his ears.

"Gross, Dad! Don't say things like that. You're going to have to pay for my therapy." Asher walked away, hands still covering his ears.

Zach laughed at Kyle's words, Zoey rolled her eyes, and Josie fought the blush that threatened to stain her cheeks at her husband's statement.

Once they were all loaded in the truck, Zoey slid over close to Zach, placing a kiss on his cheek.

"Oh God, no. Dad's talking about hot, kinky, sex with my *mom*, and you guys are practically making out in front of me.

For the love of all that's holy, please stop." Asher groaned from the extended cab.

"I think Dad's words are a bit more damaging than you seeing me kiss my boyfriend's cheek, little brother. We're dating, get used to it." Zoey snipped back.

Looking up at Zach, she smiled.

"Thanks for the flowers and card."

"What flowers and card?" Zach replied somewhat guiltily.

"The flowers and card that were in my front seat when I left work." Zoey sat up from Zach's chest as they drove down the road.

"Sorry, Zoey, I didn't do flowers and a card. Now I feel like an ass for not doing them. But the ones in your car weren't from me." Zach felt a stab of annoyance at whoever had given his girl flowers.

"What did the card say?" Zach questioned.

"To the most beautiful girl in the world. Happy birthday." Zoey worried her bottom lip.

"Who else would give me flowers and a card like that, Zach?"

"One guess, Zo. His name starts with *douche* and ends with *bag*." Zach spit the words out, knuckles white as he gripped the wheel.

"Jason? I didn't even think about him. I was thinking family members. But, you're right, flowers and a card is totally something Jason would do. And early too, sort of like he's beating you to the punch." Zoey nodded her head slowly as she thought over the thought that Jason was the sender.

"Yep, good ol' Jason. My favorite asshole to hate." Zach just shook his head.

"Well, I'll take the flowers to work on Monday and leave them to decorate the front desk. I don't want them at the house. And the card can find its way to the trash."

Leaning over to kiss him again, Zoey whispered, "Forget about him. Let's have a nice night."

"Good God, get a room!" Asher groaned from the backseat.

Zach and Zoey just laughed, and then added a bit more tongue than necessary just to really mess with the kid.

By the time they arrived at the guys' house, Zach and Zoey had played up the kissing so well that Asher had assumed the fetal position in the back of the truck.

Rushing from the vehicle, he barged into the house.

"Save me, they've been making out all the way over here." Throwing himself on the couch, he kicked his shoes off, and grabbed a handful of carrot sticks.

"One day, young grasshopper, you too will find delight in the power of a girl's tongue." Kendrick bowed in front of him.

"Or a boy's. I'm just sayin'." Sawyer piped up.

"Tongue good. Very, very good. Girl tongue, boy tongue, all tongue." Kendrick continued to play it up.

"Stop, stop. No tongue." Asher laughed at the guys.

"Someday you'll be begging us for kissing advice. In fact,

mark my words, kissing a girl *or a guy*, will be on the top of your list within a year. And you'll be all like, 'Please, give me tips. Tell me what to do.'" Kendrick grabbed Asher in a head-lock and ruffled his hair.

"No way, I'm not kissing anyone. Boy or girl." Asher, shook his head emphatically as he headed to the kitchen for more food.

Kendrick and Sawyer just smirked at each other as they watched their youngest cousin leave the room.

"Within the year. Guaranteed." Kendrick whispered.

Sawyer nodded in agreement.

AFTER SEVERAL HOURS OF FOOD, games, movies, and fun, it was nearing time for Asher to head home.

"Katie and I can take him home, I'm actually going to spend the night over at her place. We have some stuff to work on." Decker offered.

"Only if you agree that by 'stuff to work on' you mean wild, monkey sex." Kendrick's eyes were already fairly glassy.

Zach stood to gather up trash, and felt his head spin. Stumbling, he caught himself on the corner of the couch.

"Whoa, there lover boy. You been drinking too much punch?" Kendrick asked.

"You spiked the punch?" Zach willed his head to stop

spinning. "Of course you spiked the punch. Damn it, Kendrick, you could have warned me."

"It's a party. There's punch. I'm in attendance. It's a given I'll be spiking it." Kendrick shrugged. "No worries though, I told Asher he had to drink from a separate bowl."

Looking over at Zoey, he noticed she was much more giggly with Aly than usual.

All of a sudden, everything seemed funny to him as well.

Sawyer and Luke grabbed their platters from the kitchen.

"We're actually going to sleep at Luke's tonight. We're heading to that festival tomorrow. Since it's out of town, we'll be getting up earlier than most of you." Sawyer spoke to the room of people who were all in various states.

Aly popped up from the couch.

"I didn't touch the punch, I figured it was spiked. I have no desire to stay here and watch *those* two make out. Can you guys swing me by my house?" Aly looked pleadingly at Luke and Sawyer.

"Sure thing. Okay, Decker has Asher. I've got Aly. That leaves Kendrick, Zach, and Zoey here at the house." Sawyer looked at the three of them cackling their heads off in the kitchen.

"Do we feel like this is a good idea?" Luke questioned.

"Zoey's not leaving, neither are the guys. I put their keys in the lock box. I think Zach knows the combination, but not when he's buzzed. They can have their fun, sleep it off, join the living sometime tomorrow." Decker grabbed his keys and motioned Asher and Katie out the door.

Sawyer, Luke, and Aly said goodbyes which were promptly added to the long list of hilarious topics Kendrick and his fellow buzzed thought mightily funny.

"Hey, how much vodka did you put in that punch? I didn't even taste it. But, damn, I'm drunk." Zach laughed, and stumbled to the table.

"I think it would be better to tell you how much punch I added to the vodka, because there's very little punch. But I made my special recipe so it's virtually tasteless." Kendrick nodded his head sagely, which set Zoey into another fit of giggles.

"I'm so glad you made Asher drink from a separate punch bowl. The last thing I need is my barely-a-teenager little brother drinking vodka at my birthday party! Damn, that stuff was strong, I only had one glass, and my teeth are starting to feel numb." Zoey ran her tongue over her teeth.

Standing abruptly, Zach grabbed her around the waist.

"Mmmmm, let me check those teeth for you, pretty girl."

Lowering his head he captured her mouth in a loose, but sexy kiss.

When she rocked her hips against his, he took a step backwards.

"Nuh-uh, pretty girl. None of that. I'm drunk, but not that far gone." He leaned in and kissed her again.

"Let's play a game." Kendrick announced.

"Go sit on the couch. I'll get the supplies." Kendrick ushered them out of the kitchen.

Moments later, Kendrick joined them. He spread out shot glasses, along with a pitcher of punch. When he saw them hesitate, he rolled his eyes.

"No worries, little fuck bunnies, we can do tiny shots. We aren't driving, no kids here to corrupt. Let's drink." Kendrick poured everyone a shot, his full to the brim.

"Okay, object of this game is to name something that sucks. I just made it up. It's the Suck Game. If you can't name something that sucks, you drink. No, you drink every time someone names something that sucks. Ready? Let's go!"

"Um, this game?" Zoey ventured.

"Correct! Drink!" Kendrick laughed.

"Um, papercuts?" Zach offered.

"Correct! Drink!"

After about 3 rounds, neither Zach nor Zoey had any idea what was going on. Kendrick kept mumbling, but he'd finished the punch. All three of them were beyond buzzed, they qualified for definitely drunk.

"Fucked up heads suck. People like that suck. Dead babies suck. Saying goodbye sucks." Kendrick had rolled himself from his seat on the floor to the couch.

Grabbing the pitcher while laughing hysterically, he said, "Puking sucks. But I've got a catcher just in case."

And with that, he was out.

"Zach, I don't think I've ever been so drunk. Correction, I've been drunk twice, and this is much worse than the first time. I really need to lay down." Zoey started crawling toward Zach's room, not able to keep her direction in a straight line.

He sat on the floor and watched her crawl away from him. She reminded him of a bowling ball bouncing from side to side on a lane with bumpers. It was funny, and he started laughing. In his highly inebriated state, he fell over on the ground and continued laughing.

Seconds, minutes, hours later, he woke to an unknown sound. He was soaked to the bone in sweat, his head swam, and he couldn't recall exactly what had happened to place him on the floor. He couldn't recall ever being as drunk as he was at that exact moment. *Damn Kendrick and his drinking game.* Standing, he stumbled to his room, and fell into bed. Darkness surrounded him, and he accepted the proffered relief from his spinning head.

Zoey's body pressed up against his. Her tiny hands ran over his torso, venturing down to grasp his steely erection. Best dream ever.

"Mmm, feels good, pretty girl."

He lifted up when her hands tugged on his shorts.

She made quick work of his shirt, then her hot little mouth was on him. He was in heaven, or hell, and he didn't want to wake up.

"Kiss me, Zach." She rolled to her back, and pulled him to her.

He moaned into her mouth, tasting her tongue, nipping her lip.

His skin was on fire, burning even hotter where their bodies touched.

"Where are your pants, pretty girl?" He asked as he tried to make sense of why she was in his bed with no pants on. Because it's a dream, stupid.

"Spilled punch, took them off." She kissed him again, palming his heat in her hand. "Take my clothes off, Zach."

"Not safe, even in dreams." He spoke the words, meaning them, but his hands reached to the hem of her shirt, and pulled it over her head.

He was clearly dreaming, because Zoey was in front of him with not a stitch of clothing. No panties, no bra. Just a swollen red mouth, a heaving chest just begging to be tasted, and long legs that were screaming to wrap around him.

"Just a dream." Zach tried to shake his head, but even in the dream, his head was still swimming.

"Touch me, Zach." She guided his hand to her center, and his head to her chest.

He felt her shatter apart on his hand. Even in his

dreams, she was beautiful when she let loose. He moved his lips up her neck, nipping at her ear, before devouring her mouth.

When her legs spread to accommodate his body, he cursed that it was just a dream. *No, I need it to be a dream, this isn't what we planned on.*

But it felt so good. His length nudged at her core, and she moaned into his mouth.

It's just a dream, just go a little farther. It's not real, so it won't hurt.

"Just a little bit, pretty girl. Relax and let me move in a little more."

He barely recognized the point when he lost control completely. Her whimpers against his lips, the vice grip of her body holding him tight, he knew nothing but the desire to pump into her body.

"Oh, Zach. It's so full."

"Zo, I gotta move. Does it hurt?" He tried to lift up on his arms, but the room spun too much. Trying not to crush her, he laid his forehead down on the pillow beside her ear.

"Fuck me, Zach. Please." Her words were slurred, and they sounded so wrong coming from her innocent mouth.

From the deepest part of his brain and heart, he tried to make sense of the dream. It was all wrong.

"Not fucking, pretty girl. Let me love you." He groaned out as he began to move.

Her hips began to rock in time with his thrusts, little

breathy whimpers filled his bogged-down head, and then her body shattered around his.

With no warning, his body exploded, and he passed out into a deep, dreamless sleep.

ROLLING OVER, Zach cracked one eye open in hopes of fending off the hangover. As his body and mind came to, he thought back on the night. Zoey's birthday party, drinking way too much with Kendrick. His mind was screaming about something else, but he let the headache block it out. Mostly.

Stretching a leg out, he ran into a warm, soft body.

In a move quick enough to give him whiplash, he rolled his body over, and found his beautiful girl stretched out beside him. Gently lifting the sheets, he confirmed they were both naked. The stain of blood on his sheet, and on his body, put a nail in the coffin of any hope he had.

"No, no, noooooo." His heart broke. "Dear God, noooooo. Not like this."

"Zach, what's wrong? Not like what?" Zoey rolled over.

"Zoey, I'm so sorry, baby. This was a complete and total mistake. It never should have happened." Zach climbed from the bed, stumbling to the bathroom.

By the time he'd emptied his bladder, and his stomach, he dragged his broken heart back to the bedroom.

Zoey was quickly gathering up her clothes.

"Zoey, what are you doing. We need to talk about this." He tried to stop her, but she threw his hand away.

Walking into the bathroom, she closed the door most of the way. He heard water running, and assumed she was washing the evidence of their ill-fated night together from her body.

"There's nothing to talk about, Zach. We got waaaaay more drunk than we should have, had sex, not sure if it was good or not, and then I wake up to you talking about what a mistake it was." Zoey's eyes glittered with tears when she walked out of the bathroom.

"Zoey, stop. You know I don't mean *you're* a mistake. I meant us having sex. It wasn't supposed to happen this way." Zach grabbed his hair in two fistfuls, and growled.

"God, KENDRICK! I'm going to kill him. He pumped us full of vodka all night." He started toward the door.

"Zach, stop. Let him sleep it off." She pulled her clothes back on, trying to run her fingers through her matted hair.

"Eww, I think I puked in my hair during the night." She walked to check the trashcan. "I made it *mostly* in the trashcan."

She looked at him and snapped, "Sorry, it was a mistake."

"Zo, stop, this is probably not a good time for us to be having this discussion. We're both fighting hangovers and probably still drunk." He walked over to her and pulled her into a hug.

"I love you, Zoey. *You* are not a mistake. *You* are my life. We can talk later, okay? Go home, drink a ton of water, take some aspirin, grab a hot shower, then sleep until you wake up." He rested his forehead against hers.

When he spoke again, his words were choked. "Baby, I'm so sorry. That was supposed to be soft, and slow, and beautiful, but it was drunk, sweaty, fast, and neither of us can remember most of what happened. I took your virginity, in a drunken stupor." He swallowed the tears that threatened. "Oh, God, baby. I could have hurt you. *Shit,* Zoey, we didn't use a condom. At least I'm pretty sure we didn't."

Zoey took a deep breath.

"Zach, this morning after scene couldn't have gone worse if it had been scripted. The only thing we have going for us is we love each other. I'm sorry for overreacting when you said it was a mistake. We both fucked up. Kendrick fucked up. Tonight, let's talk this all out. It will be better when we aren't hungover. And after we talk, we can talk to Kendrick."

Once Zach had fiddled with the lock box and gotten keys out, he handed his truck keys to Zoey. "Here, drive my truck home."

"No, I think my body could do with some fresh air and exercise."

With kisses, hugs, and promises of love, they parted ways.

But Zach damn sure wasn't waiting until later to talk to Kendrick.

Walking into the living room, he found Kendrick passed out on the couch.

"Get your ass up, mother fucker." Zach grabbed him by the shoulders and hauled his limp body to the ground.

"What the ever-loving fuck, Zach! Back off!" Kendrick rolled himself to a seated position. "Damn man, can a guy even get a piss before being assaulted in his own home?"

"Fine, go piss. Then you and I are going to have a little talk. You were part of a *major* fuck up last night." Zach motioned toward the bathroom.

"What's new, I'm always part of fuck ups. Everywhere I look, people around me are getting fucked up." Kendrick mumbled on his way to the bathroom.

While waiting on his cousin to relieve himself, Zach attempted to calm the bubbling anger threatening to explode from inside. But trying to calm down didn't work.

Kendrick didn't even see it coming. One moment, he was walking from the bathroom, the next he was holding his gushing nose, and fighting to stay on his feet.

"Damn it, Zach! I think you broke my nose." Kendrick walked to the kitchen and leaned over the kitchen sink. Grabbing paper towel, he held it against his nose in hopes of stopping the flow.

Zach paced the kitchen, eyeing Kendrick like he wanted to hit him again.

"What the fuck, man? I wake up with a headache so bad I'm thinking it must be a brain tumor, my stomach is rolling like the deep blue sea, and you're punching me in the fucking nose. Not cool, man, not cool." Kendrick spoke from behind a mask of crumpled paper towels which were quickly soaking through.

"Not cool? Not cool?! You want to know what's *not cool*, Kendrick? How about the fact that you forced so much alcohol into Zoey and me that we were *beyond* drunk and ended up taking things *way too far* last night after we went to bed. How's that for not cool?" Zach clenched his fists at his sides.

"Aww, fuck man, I'm sorry. I was just looking to drink away some bad shit, I wasn't trying to cause you and Zoey any trouble." Kendrick hung his head. "I'm truly sorry."

"Yeah, well, fix your fucking nose and sleep off your hangover. You, me, and Zoey are talking tonight. You can apologize to her." Zach spun around and left the room.

A large part of him placed every single bit of blame on Kendrick.

A very tiny part of his head and heart, a part he had no desire to give credence to, was whispering, prodding, pushing. You and Zoey chose to drink. You knew you both were already drunk, you knew that drinking game would only make it worse. This isn't completely Kendrick's fault.

He pushed aside the nagging voice, and clung to the fact that Kendrick had spiked the punch, Kendrick had introduced the game, Kendrick was the main one at fault here.

14

"Come here, pretty girl." Zach held his hand out to her, and they naturally began walking toward the park.

The silence as they walked soothed. Could anything warm his heart and soul the way simply holding her hand could? Things had to be okay between them. She wouldn't be holding his hand if he'd totally screwed it up. At least that was the hope.

The day was a perfect temperature, just a slight breeze. Reaching the park, they continued in a warm silence while both seemed to gather their thoughts.

He let her lead, following her to a small grove of trees where a low bench carved from an old log was almost completely hidden from view. Settling down sideways on the bench, one leg stretched parallel, one leg bent and touching the ground, back against the tree, he pulled Zoey down to sit between his legs.

Drawing comfort from the warmth of her body pressed against his, Zach waited. Would she want to speak first, or was she waiting on him?

"So, did you get some sleep?" She pulled his arms tight around her body and snuggled deeply into his chest.

"Yeah, I slept like the dead. You sleep? You feeling okay?" He nuzzled her ear as he spoke.

"I took some aspirin, took a shower, and slept for about five hours. I'm not feeling bad, almost human." A smile colored her answer even though he couldn't see her face.

"Listen, Zo, about last night..."

"No, hang on. I'll let you say your piece, but I need to speak first." Zoey's words were strong, her decision firm.

It was either a good sign, or a very bad sign.

"I've thought about last night a lot. While I walked home, while I zoned out in the shower, before you met up with me. And I've decided some things." She held his hands in her own as she spoke.

"Zoey..." The urge to apologize, again, for last night and the disaster from the morning after was strong.

"Zach, stop. I need to say this." She turned on the bench to face him, sitting as close to him as she could.

Taking a deep breath, she began. "You know I love you."

Shit, that wasn't exactly a strong beginning. Was she stating that fact only to let him down easily?

"Stop trying to guess what I'm going to say. I can see it in your eyes. Please just listen." She reached up and cupped his cheek.

"As I was saying, I love you. I've always loved you in one capacity or another. I don't have a single memory of growing up that doesn't somehow, directly or indirectly involve you. What we have has been perfect from the very beginning."

She stopped talking for a moment and stared at their clasped hands.

"We've been perfect 'cousins,' perfect friends, the perfect couple, and we've had this perfect plan of what would happen from one milestone to the next." She turned a small smile up towards him. "But, you know what I decided today? We aren't perfect. We're human. We mess up; we make mistakes. That doesn't change how much we love each other. It doesn't change the fact that we want a future together. It just means we're real."

When Zach started to protest, she put a finger to his lips.

"Zach, I'd rather be *real* with you than perfect. Perfect has too many expectations, too many things hidden or glossed over. Perfect is easy, safe, beautiful. *Real* is hard, scary, ugly, and it hurts sometimes. As long as you're by my side, I'll take *real* over perfect every single time." She stopped a moment to kiss him.

"But, Zoey, what happened last night..." His voice caught, fighting to scramble over the tears.

"Shhh, what happened last night is something that thousands of people have dealt with. Yes, it was messy, and not exactly what we had planned. And, this morning? Holy shit, talk about epic failure." She giggled. "But, Zach, we built our first time up so much. The whole age thing, the timing, the place...it was all just too much. We tried to keep it easy and casual, but we still made it a much bigger deal than it should have been. I mean, we have this amazing history together, the progression of our relationship shouldn't be based on dates and numbers."

When she stopped speaking, he wanted to jump in and add to the conversation, but he chose to let the words just sink in. So, she wasn't mad at their monumental screw-up? She actually was okay with it? Leave it to his girl to take something that could have been a complete catastrophe and turn it into something good.

"Really, if you think about it, based on our friendship and our past, what happened between us last night and this morning makes for a fabulous story. I mean, sweet, soft, romantic has its place and I plan on cashing in that raincheck, but you've got to admit that screwing our brains out like rabid monkeys, and not remembering much of it through our hungover stupors the next morning is pretty funny. If we weren't in a committed relationship, it would have been reckless, unsafe, demoralizing. But, last night and this morning doesn't change a single thing between us, except giving us something *real* to cherish." She smiled at him and blushed as she bit her lip. "And, now we can get down and dirty anytime we want without the huge buildup."

This girl was amazing. He shook his head and laughed, pulling her close for a kiss.

"Zoey, you are unbelievable. Last night could have totally ruined a relationship, but you..., I have no words, you're simply amazing." Tracing her ear with his tongue, he breathed her in deeply. "But, I sort of feel like I'm getting let off the hook way too easily here. Like if my dad or yours was to hear about this debacle, I doubt either of them would be as accepting. I was drunk and took advantage of you. It was wrong."

She chuckled, "Well, if your dad found out about last night, we'd probably get a very stern lecture on the dangers of alcohol and unprotected sex. If *my* dad were to find out about last night, I think he'd likely be upset, but he knows life isn't perfect, and plans don't always work the way we think they will. He of all people understands that. We didn't have some random hookup, we just moved the inevitable up by a few days. Not to mention, I was just as drunk and I was taking advantage just as much as you. We both played our part in last night's mistakes."

"Well, there's someone else who played a huge part, and he's not getting off the hook as easily." Zach stood, taking her hand, and began walking.

"Whoa, hold on there, Rambo. We are not going in, guns

blazing, and blaming Kendrick for this." She stopped and tugged on his arm.

"Zoey, he pumped us full of alcohol last night. You're not even legal, and he had both of us drinking ourselves into oblivion. Don't tell me he doesn't deserve some blame." His face was on fire, fists clenching, as he spoke of his beloved cousin. Kendrick had definitely found his way onto the Shit List.

"We are going to the house, we will talk to Kendrick. But, Zach, if you'll let go of your anger and misplaced blame, I think there's another possibly bigger issue going on with Kendrick."

As her small arms wrapped around his waist, he spread his legs to give her something solid to lean on. Not wanting to think about Kendrick, Zach leaned his head down and caught her lips with his. When she opened her mouth on a whimper, he took advantage and let his tongue trace her bottom lip before delving in to meet hers. Walking them a short distance to a nearby tree, he turned so his back took the brunt of the rough bark. Snaking one hand up the back of her shirt, while the other grasped the back of her head and tilted it so he could deepen the kiss, he moaned into her mouth when she rocked her hips against him.

Breaking apart reluctantly, he nipped at her bottom lip, letting his hands travel down her backside and pulling her tightly against the desire raging behind his zipper.

"We should get our talk with Kendrick over with, then we

can continue this matter privately." He kissed her soundly, and they turned back towards the house.

WHAT THE HELL was Kendrick doing still asleep? It wasn't like his cousin to sleep the day away, even after a rough night of drinking.

"Hey man, Zoey and I wanted to talk to you. Can you get dressed and come to the living room?" Zach poked his head into Kendrick's pitch black room. When had he added the darkening curtains?

A grumbled, garbled string of curse words was his answer, but he saw Kendrick roll over and his feet met the floor.

"We'll give you a minute to get yourself together." Had he ever seen Kendrick look so off-kilter and disheveled?

Returning to the living room, he sat with Zoey on the couch. He couldn't shake the feeling that something was wrong with Kendrick.

"You see it now too, don't you?" Zoey's voice was soft.

He nodded.

"I feel like it's been this long, drawn-out thing, like several years drawn out. I remember when I was about 11, Kendrick acted really different for a while. He wasn't as happy, not as fun. But, then it got better, or at least it seemed to. Kendrick has always been the life of the party, but recently he's been off, different, down. It didn't all come together until the family was together on Thursday night, and then again last night, but he's got something going on. It's like he slips into this weird zone where he talks about crazy stuff, then he realizes what he's done so he pops back into Kendrick mode in order to cover up his slip." She worried her lip as she spoke.

"Yeah, he's always been a master at drawing or diverting attention when needed. Whether on or off himself or someone else. I hadn't really noticed it, but you're right, he's been off lately. Do you think we can get him to talk about it?" Zach mused, but he stopped short as his cousin's likeness appeared in the living room.

Kendrick looked...destroyed, slayed, he looked like a shell of the man they both loved.

"Holy hell, man, what's going on with you? You've never had this type of recovery period from a night of drinking." Zach watched with concern as Kendrick flopped himself next to Zoey on the couch.

Holding his head in his hands, he ran fingers through his hair roughly, fisting it into clumps and pulling hard enough both Zach and Zoey winced.

"Kendrick, what's going on? Talk to us." Zoey reached over and pulled him into a hug.

A piece of his heart broke while Zach watched his tough, charismatic, smart ass cousin shudder and sob into Zoey's hug.

"Zoey, babe, I'm so fucking sorry about making you drink last night." Kendrick pulled away from her shoulder and wiped dejectedly at his tears. "You have every right to hate me, and Zach had every right to punch me."

"You punched him?!" Zoey turned shocked eyes toward him.

"What? It was before I knew we were okay, I was pissed." Turning his words toward Kendrick, he continued, "Man, I'm sorry for punching you. You played a part in last night, but Zoey and I had just as much of a part in that disaster, so I shouldn't have placed the blame all on you."

"No, you were right to punch me. I deserved it. I think I almost welcomed it. The pain of that punch helped to block out the other pain for a while." Kendrick stared at the wall, completely zoned out.

"The pain of what, Kendrick? What's hurting you?" Zoey rubbed his back as she spoke softly.

"Nothing I can talk about. Dumb mistakes as a kid. Things that were way out of my control. Lives changed, precious lives gone, hidden, pushed away. It's just hitting me harder than it usually does. I just wanted to forget, didn't want the barrage of memories and the what ifs." Kendrick scrubbed a shaky hand over his face. "But, I was wrong to try to use you guys to bury my shit. I'm so very sorry."

"Man, it's okay. Zoey and I have talked, we're good. All of us are good, no harm, no foul. I was angry and scared this morning when I yelled at you, but it wasn't right to place the blame all on you." Reaching over, Zach clapped his cousin on the shoulder. "Hey, seriously man, we're good. You need to snap out of it."

With a humorless laugh, Kendrick spoke sardonically, "Yeah, I'll just snap out of it, because that will fix everything. Maybe I should just snap out of here, go somewhere I won't bring everyone down." He stood and headed back to his room.

"I'm worried about him. Like, really worried." Zoey chewed on her lip. "Do you think Audrey and Jeremiah know what's going on? I mean, he said 'dumb mistakes as a kid', surely they would have known what was going on if he was living there."

"I don't know, Zo. But we should talk to them. Let's give him a little time to see if he peps back up, but if he doesn't, we'll ask them about it." He pulled her onto his lap. "Now, before we spend our whole evening psychoanalyzing Kendrick, let's discuss the other options available for our entertainment."

She giggled, and tried to wriggle out of his grasp when he began to tickle.

"Come on, let's order in and head up to my room. I think I'd very much like to keep you locked up in there for a loooong time." He winked, and pulled out the menus.

They decided on sub sandwiches from the local deli. Once their dinner had been delivered, and Zoey had called home to let them know she was likely spending the night at the guys' house, they settled in on his bed.

"So, Mom and Dad want me home tomorrow for birthday dinner after church, but you're invited too." She spoke around a cucumber dangling from her mouth.

Sitting cross-legged at the head of his bed, Zach knew he'd never seen a more beautiful, perfect, *real* woman. His heart ached with love for her, his body raged with desire for her.

As they cleaned up the remains of the sandwiches and chips, Zoey leaned down to dig through his Wii U games. The Xbox was downstairs, but he kept the Wii U in his room since he'd brought it from school. It had been one of his first *I'm on my own, I can spend my money how I want* purchases at college.

His eyes roamed her frame, bent over his games, and couldn't help but admire. He grinned as he thought about what they may be doing later in the evening.

"Ah-ha! That's what I'm looking for." She held Mario Kart 8 up in triumph.

"Looking to do a little racing, huh?" Zach smiled and tweaked her nose.

"Mmmm, I have a proposition for you, Mr. Morgan."

His groin ached as she walked to him slowly and ran a finger down his chest. She lifted what he supposed were meant to be seductive eyes to meet his. What was she up to?

With no warning, she busted out laughing.

By the time she'd calmed her outburst, tears were running down her face.

"Zoey, what the heck are you doing?" Digging through his games, playing seductress, laughing hysterically, he couldn't keep up with her.

"Sorry...," she hiccupped, "I was trying to play all sexy and erotic, but I can't do it. I imagined what I looked like with that cucumber hanging from my mouth, a video game in hand, trailing a finger likely still covered in grease from the chips down your chest, and I just couldn't stop the giggles. Sorry, when you fell in love with me, you totally missed out on the erotic seductress." She covered another hiccup.

Surely she didn't think he wanted anything but what she was, did she?

"Pretty girl, you have to know that you're everything I could ever want and more, right?"

"Yeah, deep down I know that. I guess sometimes I just wonder if you'd rather have someone older, more experienced, worldly." She blushed. "Not just some girl, barely out of high school, who takes classes at the local college, and teaches some classes at the community center."

He grabbed her chin, tipping it up. Moving close to her, so his breath feathered across her cheeks, he spoke. "Never. I want the innocence, the zeal, the zest for life. I want *real*. I want *you*." He pulled gently on her chin as he took another tiny step so their bodies were flush. Brushing his lips across hers, he whispered, "Now, what do you have planned for that racing game?"

Dazed from his words, his touch, his love, Zoey's eyes

stared at him blankly for a few moments. Looking down at the game in her hand, she regained her senses and blurted, "Strip Mario!"

His girl had just suggested they play video games with the very real possibility of her stripping completely naked. Hell to the yeah.

He smiled suggestively. "Let me get this straight. My beautiful girlfriend wants to play a racing game, and clothing coming off during this game is a very probable outcome?" Wagging his eyebrows playfully, he chuckled when she slowly nodded her head up and down with a sinful smile.

"Game on, Zoey Belle. Game on." With a fist pump, the competition began.

The rules were simple. If you won the race, you got a kiss. If you lost the race, you removed a piece of clothing.

Zoey was better at certain tracks than others.

"Hey, have you been playing this with Asher? Damn it, Zo, don't throw those bombs at me. Shit, fucking Donkey Kong just passed me. Wait, where are you? Hell, how did you get in first place and I'm in eighth?" Zach hated to lose, but he smiled secretively at how excited his girl was to win that race.

He removed a sock. And she cashed in her kiss.

"Let's go, loser. I've got races to win, and you've got clothes to remove."

She was so damn adorable when she talked smack.

Three laps around the beach track later, the smack talk had been shelved.

Zoey removed her pants. He stole his kiss.

"Bet you were wishing you'd kept your socks on before this little game started, huh?" He laughed at her pouty face.

As the races continued, the kisses grew longer, the clothes became fewer, and concentration became less focused.

By the time he was in only his boxers, and she was laying on her stomach totally naked, he knew the game was over. Pressing pause, he removed the controller from her grasp. Lowering his weight so he was partially on the bed, partly on her, he wrapped arms around her.

"Game over, pretty girl."

The shiver that ran through her body ignited his even more.

"I'd say I hate to lose, but I don't think there's going to be any losers in this game." Turning so her back was against him, she rubbed her backside against his obviously interested erection.

"Arms up, baby. Clasp them behind my head. Don't move them." He growled in her ear. As his hand traveled tortuously down her body and back up, he continued his assault of words. "No vibrator, no whip cream, no drunken fog. Tonight it's just you and me, my body on you, in you, making you mine."

Arching her back, she tried to free her hands from behind his head, but he held them tight with one hand.

"I'm going to touch every single inch of your beautiful body and follow with my tongue." He made his promises as his hand continued its exploration. Eyes closed, senses on overload, he reveled in the swell of her breasts in his hand, the soft curve of her waist, the slight indent of her naval.

Her whimpers almost did him in. "What do you want, pretty girl?" Teasing, he let his hand briefly skim the place he knew she wanted him most.

"Please, Zach, touch me." Before he could continue his teasing, she turned her hips slightly so that the next pass of his hand brought him in contact with where she longed for him to be. "There, touch me."

Several moments later, he knew he'd never tire of watching her come apart, and he wanted to watch it again. Rotating her so her head was on the pillows, he started a trail of kisses at her ear, tracing her jaw, spending several minutes at her lips, until her hips rocked into his.

"No, no, no, pretty girl. Nothing hard and fast tonight. Patience." He nipped down her neck, across her collar bone. Filling his hands with her breasts, he circled his tongue over and around, nipping lightly until she cried out.

Knowing exactly where his body wanted him to be, he prolonged the torture a bit longer. Moving his kisses to her inner thighs, slowly tracing his tongue around her center, he dipped momentarily into her very core, before retreating.

Her frustrated whimper was enough to make him chuckle and relent. All teasing aside, his heart and another body part swelled when she shattered for him once more.

Bringing his mouth up her body, kissing deeply into her

mouth, letting her taste herself on his tongue, he forced himself to stop. Breathing heavily, he asked, "Protection? We didn't use anything last night."

"It's all good. I got on the pill about a year ago. Mainly to prepare for this since we both knew it was going to happen, but the fact it helps my periods be lighter is a nice little side effect. We're good, assuming you're safe?"

The unsure look in her eyes stung a bit. Yes, he'd been with other women, but he'd always used protection. He'd never risk picking up something he'd later pass on to Zoey.

"I've always been careful, for you. But, I got tested about 2 months ago, and there's definitely been no one since then." He kissed her softly, wanting to portray how much he wanted to protect her.

"Then we're good to go." She quipped lightly, but then her breath caught when he rocked his hips against her core. "Oh, God, Zach. No more talking, please."

"Please, what, pretty girl?" He dragged his boxers down as he spoke, his eyes never leaving hers.

"Love me."

She opened herself to him, freely offering the only gift he'd ever longed for.

Slowly, softly, he pressed into the only heaven he'd ever need. He was home.

"Wow, we're three-for-three tonight. I think we've made up for the debacle of Friday night." She rested her head on his chest, both of them breathing heavily after yet another round. "But I think since good things come in three's, we should stop while we're ahead, and get some sleep. Church and lunch with my parents will come soon tomorrow." She glanced at the clock, "Or, it will be here sooner because it's already today."

Chuckling, he rolled to his side, cuddling her into his chest. They fell asleep immediately.

Only the offending sound of her phone alarm pulled them from sleep several hours later.

Once the annoying chime had been silenced, eyes still closed, he gathered her tightly into his embrace. "This. This right here is what I've been waiting for my entire life." He kissed the side of her head. "From the moment you were born, I've wanted you to be mine, and you always have been in one way or another. But waking up with you in my arms is like making the circle complete. You're my family, my best friend, my favorite girl, my forever. I love you, Zoey Belle."

Sighing into his chest, she lifted teary eyes to look into his. "I've loved you since the day I was born. My entire life I've wanted nothing more than to be yours. It seems so strange that we've waited so long for the time to be right, and now it is. It's almost like living in a fantasy where all dreams come true." Lifting her lips to kiss him lightly, she continued, "I love you with everything I have Zachary Malone Morgan."

Before the moment turned too heated, he rolled out of bed and grabbed a gift box from his closet. Handing it to her, he sat on the bed beside her. "Happy birthday, pretty girl."

Inside the box was the perfect gift if her reaction was anything to go by. He'd gotten her a large gift card to the local garden center so she could buy her butterfly bush, and some of the other things she'd need for her garden. The box also contained two tickets.

"Those tickets aren't to anywhere specific. We'll make plans and get the trip set up. But, be thinking about where you want to go first on our 'Zach and Zoey Tour.'"

"Thank you, Zach, I love it all so much. You know me so well."

They managed to keep their hands off each other during quick showers and arrived at church in time to meet up with the rest of their extended family.

15

"Zoey, there's a letter for you. It came yesterday." Josie spoke as she placed the roast on the middle of the table.

Zach and Asher were finishing up the ice in glasses and pouring the tea. Zoey was setting the table, and Kyle had been charged with getting the side dishes to the table.

Zach loved watching Zoey with her family. He knew they had a special situation in that he'd known her parents since before she was even born, but he loved the closeness. Images of them sharing a home, having a family, living their perfect future floated through his mind.

Until Asher stuck an ice cube down his shirt.

"Dude, you are so going down." Zach lunged for the teen.

Asher ran from the room and out the backdoor.

Grabbing the bowl of remaining ice cubes, Zach gave

chase while the other three just shook their heads and
laughed.

Having grown up around Zoey's house, Zach was aware
of the best hiding places. He also noticed that a neighbor cat
came around the side of the house like a rocket.

So Asher was hiding along the side of the house. He had
two options. Go towards him from the front, or circle around
and try to sneak up behind him. It really had been too easy,
thanks to the cat.

Deciding to make a sneak attack from behind, Zach
tiptoed around the front of the house in hopes of coming up
behind Asher. Sure enough, the kid was hiding at the back
corner of the house trying to peek his head around to look at
the backyard.

Zach got within three feet of him before Asher sensed his
presence and turned around. In shock, he tried to run but
stumbled over his feet. Zach took advantage of the younger
man being on the ground. Pouncing on top of him, Zach sat
on him in a straddle position.

"Thought you'd get me, huh? One little ice cube down
the shirt? Child's play. You're playing with the big boys now,
Ash. I hope you're ready." Zach's grin was evil, but it was all
in good fun. "You look like you could use a cool down. Here
let me help with that." He grabbed the waistband of the kid's
shorts and pulled it out far enough to dump the melty ice
right on Asher's groin.

Asher screamed, laughing and kicking, as the ice made contact with his skin.

"Ahh, how's that feel, buddy? Nice and invigorating, huh?" Zach held the boy down so the ice wouldn't fall out of his shorts.

"Hey, boys?" The sound of Zoey's voice caught them both off guard. Turning towards her, they attempted to protect themselves, but the icy cold water blasted from the hose and soaked them within seconds.

She laughed as they scrambled to run away from her. Luckily for them, the hose didn't have much length, so she was tethered.

Smiling sweetly, she simply stated, "Lunch is ready. Mom wants you to come eat."

Asher waited until she put the hose down, then walked awkwardly towards the door, shaking ice cubes out of his shorts on the way.

Zach walked nonchalantly toward the house, but lunged for Zoey when he was within arm's reach. Grabbing her and pulling her into a big, wet bear hug, he laughed at her squeals.

"Mmmm, you got me all wet, now I want to share it with you." He shook droplets of water from his hair.

Once they were all toweled off, the five of them sat down for lunch. Jokes, laughter, and good conversation filled the room.

When the men had cleared the dishes, Zoey grabbed the letter from the kitchen counter.

Zach watched her face light up as she read it.

"What is it, pretty girl? Something good?" He walked up behind her, wrapping his arms around her, leaning his chin on her shoulder.

"Yeah, it's something good. Very good." She turned in his arms, and spoke excitedly. "Before graduation, I applied for this trip to San Diego paid for through the school. Since the high school and the local college works together on a lot of programs, I'm still eligible for the trip because I'm in the right classes at the college. I got picked as one of ten to attend the neurokinetic therapy symposium. We will be in classes, learning background and techniques Friday through Sunday, and then staying Monday and Tuesday for sight-seeing. It's all paid for through a joint grant between the high school and college."

She stopped momentarily to catch her breath. The smile on her face was enough to make his heart soar for her.

"Zo, that's fantastic. So, what's this neurokinetic therapy? Something you can use at The Center+?" He loved seeing her so excited.

"It's a corrective movement system to address the cause of pain. It helps correct the dysfunctional movement patterns stored in the brain. It would be an amazing practice to have available at The Center+. We'd be the only location for a several mile radius with someone trained in the practice, so we'd likely get a lot of referrals coming in." Zoey spoke knowl-edgably about the therapy, and he could also see her wheels turning in preparation for how this could increase business at The Center+. His girl was so very smart, both book wise, common sense wise, *and* business wise.

"That's fabulous, Zoey. You know Decker is always looking to bring in bigger and better at The Center+ as long as it's a good practice. And it sounds like you've really done your research. How did you get chosen?" They walked to the living room to find Kyle and Josie.

After she caught her parents up on the trip and therapy, she continued. "Well, they listed the top students from the qualifying classes at both the high school and college. GPA, community involvement, teacher and professor recommendations, and the essay we wrote on the application for the trip, they figured all of those things in and chose the top ten."

After hugs and congratulations were given, Zach and Zoey headed over to the guys' house to tell them the good news.

"Thanks for being okay with this, Zach." She nibbled her lip.

Looking at her in confusion, he questioned, "Why wouldn't I be okay with this, pretty girl?"

"I don't know. Some of the girls who applied for the program were all worked up about boyfriends not being okay with them taking this trip with the group. I didn't expect you to balk at it, but it just reminds me that what we have is so good when you're happy for me."

"Zoey, I will always support you in everything you do. If

it makes you happy, it makes me happy. I want nothing more than you to reach your goals and be the best *you* you can be." He reached for her hand and rubbed her knuckles with his thumb.

"Do you remember the day you left for college? We were in my room, I was crying. You told me that we'd come back together when we'd both written our stories and knew who we were. I just feel really lucky that I get to have you by my side as I finish writing my story, and we write our story together. I appreciate that you encourage me to find out who I am, outside of us, outside of this town. A lot of guys aren't like you; they are jealous or try to stifle their partner's desire to learn and become more. So, just....thank you for being you, and loving me in only the way you can." She finished her words as he helped her from his truck.

Keeping her pinned against the truck seat, the open door hiding them just enough, he aggressively captured her mouth, plunging his tongue in to mate with hers. Pouring his heart into the kiss, he didn't let up until she whimpered against his mouth. Only then did he break their contact and look deep into her eyes.

"Zoey Belle, we've survived eighteen years of roadblocks, setbacks, and having to be patient. A five day trip to San Diego for you to learn something that will inevitably broaden your horizon, is no threat to us. I'm so damn proud of you, Zo." Kissing her again, he rested his forehead against hers. "Maybe it's because I got to go off and live the college life for four years, while you had to wait for me back here. But, I feel like there's no one who deserves the honor of this trip more than you. Never, ever worry that I'll try to hold you back. I don't ever want you to fly away, but you can be damn sure I'll push you to find your wings. And then I'll fly with you, wherever you want to go." He wiped her tears with his thumbs. "Now, let's go tell the crew about my hella smart girlfriend."

They were laughing as they walked in the front door, but when they saw Sawyer, Luke, Decker, and Katie sitting somberly on the couches, they stopped short.

"What's wrong?" Zach immediately reached for Zoey's hand.

Sawyer looked around at the rest of the group before speaking. "It's Kendrick. He's gone."

"Okay, we're not his babysitters, he's a big boy. Why the long faces?" Zach spoke, trying to come across like Kendrick being gone was no big deal, but he knew, deep in his heart, that Sawyer didn't mean Kendrick was out on a date or at the store.

Rolling his eyes at his cousin, Decker handed the note over. "He left this."

Dear Everyone,

I'm going to head out of town for a while. I need to be

somewhere I can try to clear my head and not bring everyone else down. Eventually, I'll let you and/or my parents know where I am, until then, please just let me be. My head is all sorts of fucked up right now. It's nothing any of you have done, it's just something from my past that's been threatening to screw me up for years, but for some reason it hit me really hard this year. My parents know a bit about the past, but they don't know everything. Know that I'm not planning anything crazy. I just need some time away. I love you all so fuckin' much it hurts, and I know you love me too. I know this will be hard for all of you, but please just let me do this.

Love,

Kendrick

He read the words several times, trying to get them to sink into his cluttered head.

Pulling Zoey with him to the recliner, he looked around at the rest of the group.

"So, what are we going to do?" He looked to Decker, knowing his cousin was the calm, controlled, planner.

"We make sure Audrey and Jeremiah know about this, and then we let it go for now. Two weeks at most, then we go find him." Decker glanced at the rest of them, looking for disagreement.

"I just wish he would have talked to us before he left. I mean, he was such a huge part of keeping me safe and hidden during that crazy stalker scenario, I wish he would have let us help him." Katie wiped at a tear and let Decker pull her close.

"I think a family gathering to talk about this would be good. That way everyone gets the same information, at the same time, and we can all be on the same page." Decker spoke with calm authority. "Zach, I'll want you and Sawyer to take over any of the work Kendrick left at The Center+, Luke can help too."

The three men nodded.

"Zoey, you looked really excited when you came in. Did you have something to share?" Sawyer, always the perceptive one, looked expectantly at her.

"Uh, yeah, I had good news, but it seems sort of silly now."

"No way, tell them. Kendrick isn't dead. He isn't dying. He just took a break. They look like they could use some good news." Zach nodded at her, encouraging her to tell them.

An hour later, after telling them about San Diego, and deciding they'd talk to Audrey and Jeremiah at the family dinner that evening, everyone went their separate ways.

"Hey, pretty girl, I saw Sawyer and Luke sneaking off for a cuddly nap, would you like to partake?" He held out his hand to her.

"Um, I'm pretty sure Sawyer and Luke would prefer privacy for their cuddly nap." She smiled.

"Smart ass, I meant would you like to cuddle up for a nap with *me*?" He smacked her ass as she ran for his room.

DINNER WAS at Jack and Judy's house that evening. It felt like a dark cloud had descended on the house. Zach stood with the whole cousin crew as they spoke to Audrey and Jeremiah about Kendrick leaving.

"Yeah, he left a note for us too." Jeremiah was uncharacteristically stoic.

"It's not our place to share what happened, maybe someday he'll feel it's okay to talk about it. I've always wondered if there was more to it, I wish he'd known he could talk to us about it. But, I understand better than most what it's like to hold onto a secret, and how that secret can wreak havoc on your life." Audrey wiped at tears and let Jeremiah pull her into a hug.

After dinner, Jeremiah and Decker shared Kendrick's note with the entire family. The moms and grandmas cried; the dads and grandpas looked concerned. When the group broke up, Kyle spoke to Jeremiah for a very long time.

"Kyle knows firsthand what it's like to have no control over a bad situation." Josie spoke to Audrey. "After giving him some time, Kyle would like to speak to Kendrick."

Audrey nodded, "Yeah, Kyle would likely be a good one to talk to him. I know he lived away from here for four years, he's a grown man and on his own completely, but he'll never not be my little boy. My heart hurts because I know he's hurting. There will never come a time when I won't hurt for my children when they are hurting."

"I know. We all love that boy. We'll get him through whatever this is. No one has ever had as much support as this family." Josie wiped her eyes and hugged her cousin close.

Zach and Zoey watched their family from the edge of the room.

He knew what Josie said was right. These people, this family, no one could as for better support. Audrey had experienced it. Kyle and Josie had been welcomed with open arms and felt the love and support. Sawyer and Luke had received that support. Kendrick, when he was ready, would be loved and supported by all of them; he would get through this rough time. No doubt in his mind.

Two weeks later, the family decided to start looking for Kendrick. They wouldn't push, wouldn't demand he come home, they just needed to know he was okay.

"I hate to leave when we don't know where Kendrick is." Zoey's eyes streamed with tears.

"Hey, no tears. Kendrick would kick your ass if he thought you were giving up this trip because of him." Zach wiped her tears with his thumbs.

"You're right. Just keep me updated okay?" She picked up

her carry-on, and held his hand as they walked toward the security check-point.

They waited until the very last moment. But, all too soon, it was time for her to walk through and get to her gate.

"We made it through four years being apart, we can handle five days. Text me all day, call me anytime. Learn a lot. I know you're going to totally kick ass." Kissing her, he pulled her into a tight hug. "I love you, Zo. Have a great time. I'll be here waiting on you to come home."

He smiled as she walked away. He felt sad to know she was leaving, but so damn proud of her for getting chosen for the trip, and for always wanting to broaden her horizons and learn new information.

Had he seen the evil grin on the face of the man who also watched her walk away, he would have felt nothing but pure fear.

16

Zoey: Oh my gosh, we have to wait before we take off because some lame ass bought a last minute ticket. So, instead of taking off early because all tickets were accounted for, we're having to wait.

Zach: Hope he doesn't sit next to you, you might claw his eyes out. Haha. Call me when you land. Love you.

He glanced at his phone for the hundredth time in a ten minute period. He was pretty sure her plane should have landed by now. Zoey's a smart, independent, capable girl; she can handle herself getting from the airport to the hotel. After all, she's with a big group. Relax. It wasn't so much that he didn't know she could handle herself, he just wished he was there to make things easier on her. This trip will be good for

you both, especially for Zoey, she needs to be on her own and
spread her wings a little here and there.

Looking back at his computer screen in hopes of getting
some work done, he pretended not be anxious for her to call.

About five minutes later, his phone buzzed. *Finally.*

"Hey, pretty girl. How was the flight?"

"Pretty uneventful after the late passenger boarded. The
whole group rented a van to get to the hotel. The weather is
gorgeous, the hotel is fabulous. We are going for an early
lunch, then we start our first session." The excitement in her
voice traveled through the phone line.

He heard voices in the background, and Zoey tell them
she'd catch up with them in a couple minutes. "Just order me
water to drink."

"I won't keep you long, Zo, sounds like the group is
heading out. Who all got to make the trip?" Zach didn't know
many of her high school friends, but he was on a first name
basis with a couple of the students in her college classes.

"Ugh, now that they've walked away, I can tell you. So,
Suzanna and Andrea from high school are here, and a couple
kids I recognize from college, but I don't know their names.
But, get this, *Jason* is here. It's not like I hate the guy, but he
was so pompous and irritating when we saw him on our
weekend trip. And the flowers, if they were from him, were
just too much. I'm sort of hoping we avoid each other, but I
almost look forward to meeting up with him and telling him
the flowers were out of line."

He tried to laugh at her flustered voice, but all he could think about was the fact douchebag Jason was spending the next five days with his girl. It didn't sit well with him.

"He says it was a last minute decision for him to attend. He actually was on the waiting list, which I'm sure wasn't great for his ego, but someone dropped out so he was just informed last night. Hey, listen, I'm going to go ahead and hang up so I can catch up with them for lunch, and then have a group to sit with at the session. I'll call you tonight. Love you bunches."

"Still my forever girl?" He smiled into the phone.

"Always."

"Oh my gosh, I know I've gushed about it every time I've called, but you wouldn't believe how much I've learned at this symposium. I know I'll be able to really help people once I'm licensed."

He heard her struggling with something on the other end of the line. When she dropped the phone and cursed, he just laughed and shook his head.

"Sorry about that, I'm trying to get my shoes on. Listen, I wanted to let you know, I'm going to eat dinner with Jason. The rest of the group is going to be drinking in one of their rooms. Since the last time I got drunk didn't turn out so pretty, and because I don't want to be flying home with a hangover, I agreed to grab some food with Jason. He's been okay the whole trip, not too annoying. I think we're going to a little sushi place just down from the hotel. I've never had sushi, and *of course* Jason is an expert in it, so he said he'd introduce me to it."

"I just bet he did." Zach tried to keep the irritation out of his voice.

She laughed softly. "I've got to eat, and I'd rather not be alone. Better the devil you know that the devil you don't, ya know? Besides, there's a burger place next door if sushi is a total bust. Listen, I'm going to talk to you while I walk to meet up with him."

"Okay, sounds good, I'll never complain about getting to hear your voice. Just promise me you won't let Jason and all of his sophistication woo you. And when his sushi dinner doesn't impress you, remember I'll take you for a burger, fries, and shake anytime."

He heard her open a door, then her voice echoed when she spoke again.

"Sorry, I'm taking the stairs down, the elevator was taking much too long." Her heels clicked down the stairs. "Oh, excuse me."

"What?"

"Nothing, I just about ran smack dab into someone on the stairway. Hey, listen, my flight leaves tomorrow at..." Her voice scrambled, then dead air.

"Zoey? Zo? Can you hear me? I think you lost me." He

waited, hoping she'd pick up signal again, but eventually he had to accept she'd lost signal.

When she didn't call right back concern niggled at the back of his head.

Zach: *Hey, give me a call or text me to let me know you got to the restaurant okay. You must have lost signal in that stairwell.*

Ten long minutes later, he was in a full-blown panic. She should have called or texted. Maybe her phone had just died. But, Zoey always made sure her phone was charged, especially when she was going out.

Swiping his thumb across the screen, he redialed her number. It didn't go straight to voicemail, which made him think it wasn't dead. *Why in the hell wouldn't she answer? Surely, even if she'd already met up with Jason she'd answer just to let him know she was okay.*

He had a sick, prickly feeling crawling across his skin.

Jason.

His phone rang.

"Zoey, damn, pretty girl, you had me worried."

"Zach, listen, it's Jason. Zoey's been hurt. I called 911, but I knew you'd want to know." The breathless voice on the line immediately put Zach into fight mode.

"What the hell did you do, fucker?" Zach was pacing the

living room by this point. With thousands of miles between them, he'd never felt so helpless.

"Man, listen, I know you don't like me, but I need you to listen. Hang on, the paramedics are here. Let me call you back. I need to talk to the police too." The line went dead.

Nausea rolled through him, fear dropped him to the floor. Gulping for breath, he fisted hands in his hair. Five minutes passed, then ten. Time may as well have stood still.

Decker and Katie walked in and found him in tears, on the floor, gripping his phone like it was a lifeline.

"Zach, man, what's wrong?" Decker's concern was immediate.

"Zoey's hurt, Jason called, but the paramedics and police showed up. Said he'd call back." The words were hollow as he spoke them.

Decker grabbed the phone and hit redial. Pressing the speaker button, he laid the phone on the coffee table.

"Sorry, man, I didn't think it would take that long." Jason appeared to be speaking as he got in his car, a door slammed. "I'm following the ambulance to the hospital."

"This is Decker, Zoey's cousin. We've got you on speaker phone. Can you tell us what happened?" Decker clapped a hand on Zach's shoulder and pulled Katie close.

"We were going to meet for dinner. But, I thought it would be nice to walk Zoey instead of meeting her. When I saw the elevator was taking forever, I headed down the stairs. I had hoped I'd get downstairs before her, or at least catch up with her if she'd gotten a head start. As I continued down the stairs, I heard a scream, but it was far below me. I didn't know it was Zoey, but the scream freaked me out so I ran down the next ten flights. There was some guy, dressed in all black, straddling her." Jason took a shaky breath.

If Zach clenched his jaw any harder trying to fend off tears and vomit, he'd bust his teeth into pieces.

"Go on." Apprehension was clear in Decker's voice.

"My first thought was that he was trying to rape her, but as I took the last flight of stairs, I saw he was just sitting there. I slowed down, hoping to surprise him. He must have been totally zoned out, because I made enough noise to wake the dead running down those stairs, but he didn't even seem to notice. He was just sitting on top of her, stroking her face. He kept saying, 'I'm so sorry I hit you, I didn't mean to. I'd never want to mar that beautiful face. I'll take such good care of you.' Zoey was out of it, the hit he landed must have knocked her out, or she hit her head. I jumped down the last couple stairs and knocked him off her. My first concern was checking on her, and while I checked to see if her head was bleeding, he scrambled around us. He all but fell down the stairs and ran out the emergency exit." Jason paused to catch his breath.

"I'll be at the hospital soon if my GPS is correct. The police want to talk to me more. They sent officers out the same door that asshole ran through. Listen, I don't know if they'll let me in to see her, because I'm not family, but since she's thousands of miles from home, maybe they'll make an exception. If you want to look into a getting a flight out here, go for it, but you may want to let me see what information I can get before you do. If it's just a bump on the head, she may be okay to fly home tomorrow." Jason was running now. Sounds of the hospital filled the air as the three of them waited with baited breath.

"Call me back in 30 minutes if I've not called you first. Zoey was coming to a bit as the paramedics loaded her up, so she's probably awake by now. Let me see if I can get some more information."

THIRTY MINUTES MAY HAVE WELL as been a thousand years. In that time, Decker and Katie called the rest of the family to fill them in. Everyone met up at John and Cindy's house, coffee and tea were prepared, hugs and prayers were shared, and worry was etched on the faces of each and every member of the family.

Sawyer started checking flights, but the earliest flight to San Diego wouldn't get Zach out there until Tuesday night. The older men convinced him to hold off on flying out there until they heard back from Jason.

Kyle and Josie went to the other room and called the hospital in hopes of offering identifying information so they could get details from the doctor about their daughter's condition.

Jason called back.

"The good news is, she's settled in a room. She's awake, she didn't hit her head hard enough to cause concern. They expect she'll be released within an hour or two. If her parents can get through and give me permission, they said they'd work something out so I can go in and see her." Jason's voice was scratchy and echoed as he paced the waiting room.

"The bad news is, the police located the guy. He ran from them. Ran straight into traffic. He's dead. The officer I talked to said they'd be contacting Torey Hope police with his identification. They wouldn't give me a name until next-of-kin are notified. But, the police said his license showed a local address. They feel it's too coincidental that a young girl from Torey Hope was attacked in the stairwell of a hotel in San Diego by a man also from Torey Hope. I couldn't give them any information about anything weird, so they will definitely want to talk to Zoey and the family. They'll be in contact, probably within a couple hours. Jesus, I'm so sorry about all of this." Jason let out a heavy sigh.

"Listen, Jason, you know I'm not your biggest fan. Never have been. But, if I can't be there with her, I'm glad she has you there. Do what you can to get in there to see her. And have her call me as soon as she can. I'm glad the fucker who attacked her is dead, or I'd be killing him myself."

Jason disconnected, and the family sat around waiting. Uncertainty and fear coated the walls of the room until each member of the family felt suffocated by it.

HE'D NEVER BEEN so lost. Hot anger threatened to boil over, but the fear coiled in his gut was actually the stronger of the two emotions. His best friend, his favorite girl, his heart was lying in a hospital bed thousands of miles away while he sat on the couch uselessly waiting on the phone to ring.

The door opened. The room stilled, as all eyes took in the new arrival. Kendrick stood momentarily in the doorway, looking as if he'd been run over and left for dead. When his eyes landed on Zach he made a beeline to him, pulling him off the couch and into a deep hug.

The tears Zach had attempted to quell began again, and he sobbed into his cousin's chest.

"She's hurt, and I'm not with her, man. I feel like I'm being eaten alive from the inside out." Drawing a shuddering breath, Zach stepped back a bit. "You look like hell."

Some anxious, awkward giggles flitted around them.

Audrey walked to Kendrick and let herself be engulfed in her son's embrace.

"Momma, don't cry. You know what this is about. I just need some time. I'll get through it, I always do." Kendrick kissed the top of her head.

"But it needs to end, baby boy. You need to open up to us, to your family, to a professional so you can move beyond it. It's getting worse over time. Please promise me." Audrey dried her eyes.

"I'll try, but I won't promise anything. I don't want to let you down if I can't follow through." Kendrick turned to his dad and let Jeremiah hug him tight.

"Zoey will be glad to know you're home." Zach clapped him on the back.

"Well, I'm not staying..." Kendrick trailed off as those in the room gasped.

"What the hell, Kendrick. Zoey is hurt, she's been attacked, and you can't stay?" Zach's temper flared.

"I came home so I could talk to her on the phone, and I'll see her soon. But, Zach, I need you and everyone to understand, I just need some time. I won't stay gone forever, I just need you to give me this." Sadness filled Kendrick's eyes.

The phone rang as Kyle and Josie walked back into the room.

"Jason?"

"Yeah, man, it's me. The call came through from Zoey's parents, the nurses are taking me back to see her. As soon as I'm in her room, I'll hand the phone over to her." Jason's footsteps sounded on the tile floor as he made his way to Zoey. "I did get to talk to the doctor. He doesn't feel comfortable releasing her tonight, and he doesn't want her on a crowded airplane. He agreed to release her tomorrow if her exam goes okay, and he will allow her to fly on a private plane. My father has a plane, well, one of his associates has a plane, and I'm going to make some calls to get it out here so Zoey can be home tomorrow."

Relief coursed through his body, but it was quickly hampered by the overwhelming need to talk to Zoey. Once he heard her voice, he'd be able to breathe easier.

Muffled voices, and a rustling of the phone sounded. Everyone in the room gathered around the phone as it was put on speaker.

"Zach?" Zoey's voice came through crystal clear. She sounded tired, but overall she sounded good.

Emotional tears, ranging from relief to fear to joy streamed down cheeks.

"Hey there, pretty girl. How are you feeling?" His voice caught. He had to be strong, for Zoey. He couldn't let himself give in to the fear, she had to know he was right there with her.

"I'm tired, shaky. *Really scared.*" As she whispered the last part, he heard the tears in her voice.

"Ah, baby, I'm so very sorry. I want so badly to be there with you. But, the earliest plane to get me out there isn't as good as getting you back here. Jason's working on a private plane to get you back to Torey Hope. Everyone is here, praying and waiting on you to get home. We'll get through it. Still my forever girl, right?" With no conscious thought as to the rest of the people in the room, he husked out his words hoping to bring peace and comfort to her.

Crying freely now, Zoey whispered back, "Always your forever girl." On a shuddery breath, she laughed lightly. "I guess when I said I wanted the *real* with you, I got my wish, huh?"

Zach laughed through his tears. That was his girl, finding something to smile about, even in the worst situations.

"Hey, I've got good news for you. Everyone is here, you can talk to your mom and dad in just a second, I think even Asher wants to say hi. But, there's someone else here too." Zach handed the phone to Kendrick.

Thumbing the phone off speaker, Kendrick spoke quietly, "Hey there, Zoey Belle. So, I hear your day pretty much sucked." He smiled slightly, closing his eyes as if to bask in the sound of her voice. He stood, listening seriously to whatever Zoey was saying. "I hear ya, Zo. I do."

Handing the phone to Josie, Kendrick motioned his cousins into the kitchen.

"Once she's home, text me and I'll come visit. I don't want to leave you guys, but it's something I need. My head isn't on straight right now, and I'm afraid if I can't get things worked out it's only going to get worse. I love you all, you're my best friends and my family. I know you don't get what's going on, but it means a lot that you're here to support me without pushing me." Kendrick slumped against the kitchen counter.

"Kendrick, we love you too. We'll give you some time. We'll support you. But, there may come a time when we *are* going to push you because we *do* love you so much." Decker made this comment in a way that sounded like both a promise and a threat.

"Fair enough." Kendrick nodded.

BY THE END of the night, a rough plan was in place to get Zoey home. Zach would have never believed he'd be thankful for Jason being with Zoey, but he truly owed the man.

The police came by. They wanted Zoey to come to the station and make a statement once she was home, or they'd come by her house if she wasn't feeling up to it.

It was a hard conversation to have, and Zach was grateful at the moment that Zoey wasn't there to hear it. He wanted her to heal and feel less scared, if possible, before hearing about her attacker.

Officer Ramsey accepted the cup of coffee offered, and waited for the group to gather around. "I'm very sorry about the trauma your family has suffered today. I'm sure you're anxious to get Ms. Martin home. We made an initial visit to the attacker's home as soon as we were contacted by the authorities in San Diego. I have to tell you, it's clear that the man, his name was Vincent Durgess, had been watching Zoey for quite a while. He moved to a neighboring town about five years ago, good neighbor, no troubles. Took several substitute teaching jobs throughout the area. When he was reported several times, by multiple sources, as making the students he was teaching feel creeped out, he was let go from the substitute position. He lost his income, along with the benefits which were providing for his medication to treat several mental conditions. When he was no longer able to treat the conditions, it appears he pretty much lost it, went off the deep end. He must have subbed at Zoey's school, we'll confirm that with the school records tomorrow. But, it appears from journals that he developed an extreme emotional attachment to her. He moved to a small house in Torey Hope, and pretty much set up a shrine to her." Officer Ramsey paused to sip his coffee.

When the group gathered around him looked sick over this news, he continued. "We will do a more thorough investigation, but we've read through quite a few of his journals. Even though what happened today was traumatic, and he was in the wrong, I want to assure you we don't believe Mr. Durgess was out to harm Zoey. He wrote of wanting to protect her, help her, make her smile. Honestly, the person he seemed the most angry with, the one he wanted to hurt, was Zach. He had several detailed pages of how he planned to do away with Zach, so Zoey would be free to be with him. From what the police are able to tell us from the site of the attack, and from Jason's information, Mr. Durgess was in an extreme state of panic and duress when he ran from the scene. The reporting officer does not feel like Mr. Durgess ran into traffic on purpose, he reports that the attacker seemed 'completely out of his mind,' and his death will be investigated but appears to be an extreme accident."

Officer Ramsey finished his coffee, and stood to leave. "We'll be in touch, and we'll want to talk to Zoey when she's up to it, the sooner the better. If we learn of anything new, we'll be sure to let you know."

He tipped his hat, but paused before leaving. "I have to tell you, I'm never glad when someone dies, but I hope the fact that he's no longer around will bring a bit of peace to Ms. Martin as she heals from this." Turning to Zach he continued, "And, I know you'd rather it had been you, but I have to tell you, son, after seeing Mr. Durgess' place, I don't think you'd have fared as well as Zoey did had he gotten to you first."

17

"You're going to wear a hole in the carpet if you keep pacing like that." Aly hugged him close. "I'm nervous too, big brother, but we are so lucky she's okay and wasn't hurt any worse."

"I know, Aly, I'm just dying to have her here. I know there's a probably a lot of bad that's going to come from all of this, I just feel helpless not having her here with me. It's almost like if I have her in my arms we can get through anything." Zach hugged his sister, but returned to pacing.

Zach, Aly, Kyle, Josie, and Asher were waiting at the small airfield outside of Torey Hope. Jason's father's colleague had agreed to pilot the plane out to San Diego and was set to arrive back in Illinois soon. While the entire family wanted to come greet Zoey, the doctor had spoken to Kyle and Josie at length about her recovery. It was to be expected she'd be shaky, spooked, unsure, so it was decided a small group of greeters was the best bet. Nothing could have kept Zach from being there to meet that plane.

"Zach, remember what the doctor said. Zoey may be clingy, or she may want her space. If she asks to be alone, don't take it personally. We've likely got a long way to go to get our girl through this recovery, she needs to know you're here for her, but it may be overwhelming for her at times." Kyle gritted his jaw as he spoke, his actions belying his calm words. He was just as anxious to have the girl home. "And, Aly, you and Zoey had been having a rough patch. Now would be a great time to fix that *if* Zoey is open to it, but the doctor said we have to let her go at her own pace."

"Right, we let her talk if she wants to talk, we let her be quiet if that's what she needs. Main thing, we just let her know we're here to love and support her no matter what." Josie clung to Kyle's side, every bit the picture of a mother hurting and longing for her daughter.

When the plane landed, a collective breath was held until the door opened.

Zach had expected her to look smaller, fragile, frail, but she looked exactly the same as when she'd left. He immediately noticed her eyes were sad and tired, and her cheek had a slight bruise, but she looked just like the Zoey he loved.

His brain tried to register Jason's arm around her, but his heart was frantically beating, drowning out the jealousy.

The group walked to the door, waiting on the two to enter.

Jason immediately handed Zoey off to Zach. His arms were around her before the first sobs shuddered through her chest. Nodding at Jason in silent thanks and appreciation, Zach buried his nose in her hair. For the rest of his life, the smell of hospital which drifted from her hair would haunt his senses. But she was home, in his arms; all was good.

EXCEPT ALL WAS *NOT* GOOD.

After several minutes of tearful welcomes and hugs, the group headed home. Very little was said on the ride, Zoey seemed content to snuggle into Zach's side and sleep.

When they arrived home, Asher gave his sister a hug. "I'm really sorry you got hurt. I'm glad you're home. I know Zach and Mom and Dad are here, but if you need anything let me know."

Zoey nodded tearfully.

With tears streaming down her cheeks, Aly pulled Zoey into her arms. "Zoey, I'm so very sorry for being such a pain in the ass lately. I don't know that I can even pinpoint the why, but after what happened, it doesn't even matter. You're my best friend, always have been, always will be. I'm here, no matter what. I'm going to give you tonight to settle in and relax, but tomorrow I'll be here. We can talk, cry, sleep, whatever you want. But, I won't be leaving you."

Zach hugged his sister to him, "Thanks, Aly. We love you. I'm glad you're here for her."

Kyle and Josie had taken Zoey's things to her room.

"I think I'm going to take a shower, I smell like the hospital. Then maybe a movie?" Zoey didn't move from Zach's arms, but looked expectantly at her parents.

"Sounds like a plan." Josie glanced at her daughter wrapped in Zach's arms. Blushing, but with a knowing smile, she hooked her arm with Kyle's. "So, Dad and I will take Asher over to The Captain's house. I know Janie has some food she wanted to send over, and we'll raid his movies to keep you stocked for the week."

Kyle's eyes traveled between his wife and daughter a couple times, understanding dawning suddenly. With a wry smile, he nodded, "Yeah, we'll just get that all taken care of while you shower and settle in. Probably take about an hour and a half."

When they'd left, Zoey crumbled in his arms.

"Shhh, pretty girl, it's okay. Want to talk about it?" Zach smoothed her hair, whispering softly in her ear.

"No, I just want a hot shower, warm pajamas, and a comfy couch. And I want you next to me the entire time." A weary kiss brushed across his lips. "Starting with the shower."

He gently soaped her body, lathered and rinsed her hair, and dried her in the biggest towel he could find.

"I'll get you some of Dad's sweats later, right now I just need you to hold me." Zoey sank onto the bed, seeking warmth under the blanket.

When they were curled together, dewy skin, warm from the hot shower, Zoey finally seemed to let loose the breath she was holding.

"I'm going to tell you something, you're not going to like it, but you're going to do it. For me. Because it's what I need right now. I don't know what the next hour or day or week will bring. I promise to fight through this, but this very moment you can give me exactly what I need." Beautiful green eyes looked at him expectantly.

"Anything, Zo. I felt so helpless being so far away from you. If there's something I can do for you now, just say the word and it's yours." He brushed the hair from her face and kissed her temple.

He gasped when she reached between them and gripped his already thickening length.

"I'm saying the word, and this is *mine*." Zoey giggled lightly, but the sound was off.

"Anything but that, Zo. I don't think it's a good time." His brows creased as he fought down the desire pulsing through him.

"You said anything. Zach, please. This isn't about sex, this isn't me hiding the pain. My heart and soul need to be close to you, if I could crawl into your skin, it would *maybe* make me feel close enough. Please, just make love to me. Nothing fancy, just letting me be as close to you as possible." She tipped her face up to his, kissing his lips lightly as she stroked below the blanket.

"Let it be said, I'm not in total agreement that the timing is right on this. Let it also be said, that I'm not one to turn down such an invitation from my favorite girl."

With a slight roll, he positioned her under him.

Grasping his shoulders, pulling him down to crush her, she whispered, "This. Right here. I need you as close as possible. I feel safe like this."

Opening herself to him, she whimpered as her body took him in.

They lay like that, not moving, for several moments.

"Move, Zach. Slowly." She commanded, but refused to let go of his shoulders.

Maneuvering his bottom half while letting his chest remain crushed to hers was challenging, but he managed. There had never been a more intense coupling. It wasn't sex, it wasn't just comfort, it was becoming one, healing, promising to stand together through every moment.

Zach realized quickly that Zoey was going to be clingy, and he felt relief. He hated the fact that she had anything to make her clingy, because she'd always been confident and independent, but he'd feared the doctor's warning of her possibly wanting to be alone, and he wasn't sure how he would have handled that.

As they dressed, he noticed she was shaking.

"Zo, you okay? Cold?" Rubbing his hands up and down her arms, he reached for a blanket.

"I'm just shaky. It's like I can't get warm, and I can't be close enough to you. I know they'll be okay with it, but I'm going to ask my parents if you can stay over the next few nights. Not for sexy stuff, just to hold me. I'm terrified of going to sleep, I keep seeing that stairwell." Her voice caught.

"Ahh, baby, you know I'll stay." He held her tight.

THE FIRST OF several nights of nightmares started that night.

For three weeks, Zoey spent her days locked in her room or curled on the couch, and her nights wrapped in Zach's arms as she fended off the bad dreams.

She spent the days at home with Zach or Aly. Zach did most of his work from her living room, Aly completed several homework assignments when Zoey would nap.

Kyle and Josie were right there, trying not to smother, but making sure she had what she needed. Asher took time from socializing with his friends to check in with her morning and night.

Aly and Zoey laughed, read magazines, did exercise videos, and watched movies.

Zach and Zoey watched more movies, caught up on the shows they recorded, and took long naps.

Zoey sat and made small talk with family visitors.

At night she'd curl into Zach's strong arms, kiss him, and tearfully say, "Maybe tonight will be the night I sleep with no nightmares."

She didn't leave the house, she didn't work in her garden, she was alive but true living had ceased. Sure she made all the right moves to look like things were okay, but Zach knew they weren't. At all.

During one of Zoey's afternoon naps, he shifted from her arms and left the couch. "Shhh, I'm just going to the bathroom, I'll be right back." His whispered words calmed her when she whimpered at the loss of him beside her.

Instead of the bathroom, he headed to the kitchen hoping to find Kyle or Josie. Luckily, he found both. The tension drawn on their faces mirrored what he was feeling.

"So, I wanted to talk to you guys." Zach spoke softly, not wanting Zoey to wake to their conversation.

Her parents nodded, and they all sat down around the table.

"Something's got to give. I know we are supposed to be patient with her, but that's not her. She won't talk about the attack, she won't see the therapist, she won't take the medicine, hell, she won't even leave the fuckin' house." Rubbing a hand over his face, he sighed, "Sorry. I'm just dying seeing her like this."

"We were just talking about this last night. I don't want to push her, but I'm afraid she's going to accept this as her new normal if we don't press just a little. We've all been walking on eggshells around her, but I think we need to talk to her. Let's start by getting her out in her garden, the fresh air and sunshine should help somewhat." Josie spoke through tears, not seeming completely sure of her words, but coming across confident that *something* had to be done.

"Right, I think outside first. Then we get her alone with members of the family who have suffered trauma of some sort. Just casual conversations, but have them pointedly speak of different ways they found to cope and heal." Zach pinched the bridge of his nose. "She needs to talk about what happened, get her feelings out. And I know she doesn't want to take the medicine, but she needs to realize it doesn't have to be forever. But if she could relax and sleep, maybe it would help relieve some of the anxiety. Believe me, I love falling asleep with her at night, but knowing she's afraid to close her eyes without me by her side just tears me apart."

The next day, after Aly left to go to class, Zach pulled Zoey close to him on the couch. Knowing the coming conversation was likely to be difficult, he held her tight. When her parents sat down nearby, Zach turned off the television.

"Zoey Belle, we need to talk to you." Zach rubbed her back.

"What if I'm not ready to talk?" Her chin quivered, but she spoke defiantly.

"Baby girl, your dad and I have both been through traumatic situations. I was attacked and beaten when I was pregnant with you. I know about the anxiety and fear which come from that." Josie spoke of a past life event which both Zoey and Zach were aware, but it wasn't something she talked about a lot.

"Zoey, you know I was married before your mom, and you know Izzy and the baby died. What I've not talked about a lot is the blackness that followed. I know how suffocating it can be, I know how shutting the world out, and giving into the blackness can give you the false impression of getting by." Kyle leaned forward, elbows on knees.

"Okay, so you both know what I'm dealing with. That means you should be giving me the time I need to heal, not pushing me to do something I'm not ready to do. I don't want to talk about it, I don't want to rely on medication to feel better, I'll deal with it my way." Zoey crossed her arms across her chest.

"Zo..." Zach began.

"No, Zach. I thought you were here to support me. But instead, you're ganging up on me with them, trying to push me towards something I'm not ready for." Tears fell from her eyes.

"Listen, Zoey, we all know it's hard. We're not asking you to do it all at once. We've got one small step we want you to work on. Can you try to give us one thing? Then we'll leave you alone for a little bit." Josie's voice was pleading.

"We love you, pretty girl, we just want to see you get better so you can stop being sad and afraid." Zach kneaded at her shoulders.

"Fine. I'm not making any promises, but I'll at least listen to your one request." Zoey sighed heavily, her desire to refuse their request was evident.

"Just work in your garden. You and Zach had gotten the materials to start your lasagna gardening. Get the beds built, weed what needs weeding, plant what can be planted at this time. That's all we're asking. For now." Kyle made the request, pausing expectantly to see how she'd react.

She sat quietly for a bit, blinking slowly. "I think I'd almost forgotten about my garden. I've sort of been in a fog. But, you're right, it needs work. I can do that."

Smiling slightly, she turned to Zach. "We'll start tomorrow."

As the garden beds began to take shape and fill with life, Zoey's eyes began to sparkle and fill with life as well. The smiles, genuine laughter, and spunk were fleeting, but Zach's heart soared to know they were making themselves known at all.

Over the next several days, Zoey had less-than-coincidental visits from certain members of her family. Zach sat at the kitchen table, under the guise of doing his advertising work, and listened as each family member sprinkled advice or dropped little thought nuggets into the conversation.

The Captain was first. "You know, Zoey Belle. When my

first wife died, I went down a deep, dark, dangerous spiral of despair. It took me several years to come out of that pit, and I regret the time I lost." He stood to leave, leaning over to hug her once more. "Don't let yourself get in such a deep hole that you can't pull yourself back out."

Zach let the tears flow freely as he sat at the table secretly listening to his mom, Carly, talk to Zoey the next evening.

"It's okay to be scared, Zoey. I was scared of my own shadow for several years. Without being too graphic, I was raped and beaten more times than I can count, so I know the fear and heartache you're feeling. I know it can seem endless. But it's not, sweet girl. You've got the most wonderful, loving, supportive family here for you. And, a certain son of mine loves you very much. You will get through this. If you decide to take the medicine, I'll tell you that it was very helpful for me during the short time I took it."

Zach had heard bits and pieces of the nightmare his mom endured before coming to Torey Hope and meeting his dad, but hearing her speak of the fear which haunted her was heartbreaking.

When Audrey came to visit the next night, Zach pretended to load the dishwasher in order to listen in.

"Here, I need you to take this. Hold onto it, read it, memorize it." Audrey thrust a card at Zoey.

"What is it?" Zoey asked, looking unsurely at the card marked darkly with the word *SURVIVOR*.

"It's one of the several cards I hung around my apartment

when I was going through therapy to uncover my utterly craptastic past. Yes, I had to admit I'd been a victim, but these cards helped me to remember I was also a survivor. Not just *was* as survivor, I *am* a survivor. And so are you, Zoey. I'm not going to lie to you, therapy was *hard*, but it was a necessary evil to get me through the bad shit so I could start finding the good stuff. I'm not saying you *have* to see the therapist, but I'll go with you if you want me to."

Zach marveled at the love between the two men as he listened to Sawyer and Luke visiting with Zoey. Closing his eyes, he savored the sound of her true laughter over something they'd said. They stayed longer than any of the other visitors had stayed. Zach heard the sleepiness creeping into Zoey's voice, and was glad the other two men caught it as well.

"Well, Zo, it's time for us to head out. I'm not into secrets anymore. I lived with my secret for long enough. So I'm just going to say this straight up. I get what you're dealing with, you know I do. That attack in the park was a living nightmare for me, I still deal with the after effects. Therapy helped a lot. I'm still taking a low dose anxiety medicine, and it really helps to keep the edge off the fear and jumpiness for me. I can't, we can't, *force* you to do these things, but I have to tell you that I think it would be helpful for you to at least talk to someone." Sawyer hugged her before wrapping his arms around Luke.

Before they left, Luke spoke, "Zoey, the nightmares I had

from the abuse I lived through were enough to make me not want to sleep. Exercise, martial arts, yoga, all of those things helped me to center myself, but the really freeing moment was when I told Sawyer about my past. I told him what happened, I told him about my feelings. Don't shut your family out. I'm not saying everyone needs a detailed description, but Zach is here for you. Share with him."

The final visit wasn't made in person, but when the phone rang the next night, Zoey didn't seem to be surprised it was for her.

"Well, you've pretty much run through all the family members who have had similar experiences as me. I wonder who this could be? Someone who just happens to call me and wants to offer their love, support, and thinly veiled advice?" Zoey spoke sarcastically, but Zach's chest swelled when he saw the genuine smile on her face.

"Hello?" Zoey's face brightened. "Hey, Kendrick. I miss you, when are you coming home?"

Zach frowned, impatient and bent out of shape when he couldn't hear the entire conversation. But he knew he'd forever be grateful if Kendrick helped to move Zoey along her path of healing.

"Yeah, I'll give it a couple months. But if I do this, you've got to do your part, no backing out." Zoey seemed to be dealing with Kendrick. "I get it, you need your time. But, as I've recently learned, sometimes we don't need time as much as we need love and support. You'll have your time, Kendrick,

But, once I'm done, you've got to keep your end of the bargain. I'll hold you to it. Got it?"

Zach wasn't 100% sure what they'd just agreed to, but he had high hopes it would be beneficial for both Zoey *and* Kendrick.

18

"Zach, this is important. I need to see it, and I need to hear directly from the police about my attacker. I'm working very hard to overcome this, but I need to see and hear these things before I can let them go." Zoey's strong confidence was making a comeback.

The attack had been two months ago, and Zoey truly was making strides in her recovery. She had yet to see a therapist, or take any medication, and the nightmares were still happening a couple times a week. But, she was gardening, doing yoga, and teaching a couple classes with Luke at The Center+ each week.

The college had agreed to let her take some time off, obviously feeling unwarranted guilt about the attack happening on their trip.

"Okay, Zoey, I hear what you're saying. But if you're

going to make demands, I'm going to make a few of my own. If I arrange for you to see Vincent Durgess' house and talk to Officer Ramsey, you need to talk to me or someone about what happened." Zach knew he was pushing, but he also knew she could take it.

"Why can't you just let me get through this myself? I don't need to talk to anyone. I love you, Zach, but I don't like you very much right now." Zoey stood her ground, arms crossed over her chest.

"Well, I'm pretty sure there are going to be a million times in our life when you don't like me very much, but that's life, Zoey Belle. Real life isn't like the movies, remember? In fact, I think a beautiful redhead once told me that *real* is hard, scary, ugly, and it hurts sometimes. This is one of those times, pretty girl." Zach stood his ground just as strongly as she did.

"You know I could find a way to talk to the police and find his house without your help. This blackmail scheme could completely backfire in your face." Squinting her eyes and jutting her chin out, Zoey challenged him.

"You're right, you could. And, yes, it could. But, I think you want me with you when you work through this part. And it's not blackmail, it's love, and caring, and support." He leaned in and kissed her gently. "Plus, you know I'm just as stubborn as you are, so I'm not going to give in on this."

Gritting her teeth, Zoey rolled her eyes. "Fine, set it up so I can see his house and talk to Officer Ramsey, and then I'll make the appointment."

"No way, pretty girl. Make the appointment, attend the first appointment, and *then* I'll set it all up." He worked hard to hold back the grin he was hiding. They'd had their fair share of tiny disagreements over the years, but they'd never really had a fight or reached a stalemate. He didn't enjoy pushing Zoey's emotions, but he very much liked the life and fire he saw in her as they argued back and forth.

"Arrghh!" She stomped her foot before turning on her heel and heading inside to set up the appointment. "They better be able to get me in *tomorrow*! I don't want to wait to make this next step."

He chuckled as she stormed up the stairs.

"So, looks like we made the right choice to push her along, huh?" Kyle walked up next to him and smiled as his daughter paced in front of the picture window while making the call to the therapist's office.

"Luckily, Sawyer talked the therapist he's been seeing into holding a slot open each day recently, just in case Zoey gave in and decided to call. She should be able to get in tomorrow." Zach was pleased, and very hopeful, that the therapist would be able to reach Zoey's inner fears and anxiety to rid her of the nightmares.

"And then you have to take her to see Vincent's house, and listen to the details about the man. You ready for that?" Kyle looked at him expectantly.

"I don't want her to see or hear anything pertaining to him, but I can understand her need to provide some closure.

I'll do whatever it takes for that to happen." He walked away to make the phone call to Officer Ramsey.

"Okay, mission accomplished, let's go." Zoey walked quickly from the small office on the east side of town.

"Whoa, Zo. How was the session?" Zach grabbed her hand, steering her to the local deli. "We need to eat before we meet Officer Ramsey."

"The session was what you'd expect. Me answering questions, telling what happened, talking about how I feel." She turned from him, and began studying the menu, attempting to ignore his questions.

Lunch was casual and comfortable, but the undercurrent of anxiety and tension was uncomfortable. For Zach at least.

"Zoey, I'm glad you followed through on the appointment. I hope you'll continue to go to therapy for at least a couple more sessions." As he talked he watched her face. She didn't confirm or deny if she would continue with therapy.

"What time do we meet Ramsey?" Zoey finished her sandwich and popped chips in her mouth.

Sighing heavily, Zach let it go for right then.

"We need to be there in about ten minutes, so we should head out." He held a hand out to her.

"Thank you for doing this for me, Zach." She leaned in to

kiss his cheek. "I just want to move past this, so you and I can go back to our normal lives."

"Zoey, you know I'll do absolutely anything and everything I can to help you through this, but I want you to think about the fact that our normal will forever change. Our normal used to be friendship, then our normal was waiting for each other, now our normal is dating and loving and growing together as a couple, but in the future our normal will include learning how to be married, pay our bills, raise children. Normal isn't static, it ebbs and flows like ocean waves." Zach ran a hand along her cheek.

"That was really pretty perfect, Zach. I get what you're saying. I do. But I still need to do this." Zoey smiled at him. "I'm ready for our normal to move on to happier things."

They pulled up to a small, nondescript house. Officer Ramsey was waiting on the sidewalk.

"Miss Martin, Mr. Morgan, it's good to see you. Miss Martin, I want to thank you for the information you were able to give us. Are you sure you want to see this place and hear about Mr. Durgess?" Officer Ramsey held his hat in his hands.

"Yes, Officer. I really need to hear about this man and see where he lived so that I can close this chapter of my life." Zoey nodded.

"Okay, let's go."

They entered the dim, musty home. Officer Ramsey flipped on the lights.

"We've done a complete sweep of the whole house. There was nothing really of interest until we reached his spare bedroom. That's where he kept his notebooks and all things pertaining to you, Ms. Martin." The officer seemed to hesitate, not sure how much to share with her.

"We've not told her anything about the attacker other than his name and the fact that he's dead. She wants to hear the details, she's strong enough to hear them, and I'm with her. She or I will let you know if the information is getting to be too much. Go on." Zach led Zoey to a stool, and took his place behind her, his arms holding her tight.

"So, most of the information we gathered came from our initial search of his home and background check. Vincent Durgess was a substitute teacher in Torey Hope and surrounding towns, he was let go after several students reported him making them feel uncomfortable. We know he subbed at Zoey's school, so we are assuming that's when his infatuation with her began. He moved to Torey Hope, but couldn't pay for his medications. His mental illness got out of control. We've combed through his notebooks. He wrote of his plans to take you away from Zach, take you to see the world, marry you, and make you happy. He wrote of following you guys when you went on a weekend trip, he's obviously been in The Center+ at least a couple times because he refers to seeing you in the studio after class. He was extremely excited when he was able to leave you flowers before Zach got you anything. He wrote of how it showed he'd be a better boyfriend." Ramsey stopped to gauge Zoey's reactions.

"So how did he know I was going to California?" Zoey shuddered.

"We don't think he knew. He wrote in his journal while he was on the plane. He wrote about following you two to the airport, and how he was ready to put his plan into action to end Zach, but when he realized you were getting on the plane, he hurriedly bought a ticket at the last minute in hopes of getting you alone in San Diego. He had a few credit cards, he used the one he hadn't maxed out yet."

"Oh my God, he was the late passenger we waited on before takeoff." She held a shaky hand to her mouth.

"He tried getting a room at the hotel where you were staying, but they were filled because of the symposium. So he basically just hid out in the stairwell and alley the best he could, waiting for glimpses of you. He had written in his journal the morning of the attack that he was going to hide in the stairwell until he saw you so he could talk to you, he was planning to ask you to dinner." Ramsey patted Zoey's hand. "Ms. Martin, you have to remember that Mr. Durgess was a very sick man. None of what he did or planned was rational. From his writings, we believe he thought he could get you to fall in love with him, then he was going to kill Zach and be there to comfort you."

"He wrote about killing Zach?" Tears sprang to her eyes.

"He wrote of it often, but never with much detail. He had

the desire, but no real plan from what we can gather." The officer shook his head as he spoke. "In a sane, rational state, we don't have any reason to believe Mr. Durgess would have followed through on his idea to kill Zach. But, with his altered mental state, we feel that he was likely capable of carrying out a murder."

Closing her eyes, Zoey leaned heavily into Zach.

He held her, waiting to see if she would speak. When she didn't, he prompted her.

"Do you want to see the room he kept his collection of things pertaining to you, or is hearing the story enough?"

"Part of me doesn't want to see it, but I feel like I've got such a terrible image of it in my head, I'm likely imagining it worse than what it is. I think I need to see it." Zoey stood and waited for Officer Ramsey to lead the way to the closed door.

When the door swung open, Zoey stood still as a statue just staring into the room.

With tentative steps, she entered the room. Wordlessly, she reached behind her to grabbed Zach's hand.

Stopping midway into the room, a choked giggle erupted from her.

"I think I've watched too many cop mystery shows. I was expecting candles, decapitated dolls, dripping blood...this is just a room."

"Most of his 'collection' is in the form of boxes and scrap-books. He seemed to suffer from some severe OCD tendencies, he kept everything meticulously neat." Ramsey led them to the desk, and opened one of the scrapbooks.

Her gasp caught both men by surprise.

"Oh! I know him, I mean, I recognize him. He *was* a sub in a couple of my classes. Oh my God, this is all so surreal." Zoey slowly skimmed through the scrapbook.

"Zach, I need you to take me one more place." Zoey quickly closed the book. "Officer Ramsey, thank you very much for sharing your information with me, and for showing me the house. I really appreciate it."

"Glad to help, Ms. Martin. Let me know if there's anything else I can do for you."

"YOU'RE SERIOUS, AREN'T YOU?" Zach picked his jaw up from the floor.

"Yeah, I am. I know it's weird, but I have this over-whelming need to do it. But, swing me by that little grocery on the way." Zoey seemed sad, but determined to finish the mission she'd set out on.

Thirty minutes later, Zach pulled the truck up to a gate. Killing the engine, he turned to her. "Can I at least come with you? I won't hover, but I'll feel better knowing I'm there in case you get upset or freaked out."

"Yes, please. I need to do this, but I need to have you with me. Just please don't laugh at me or judge what I need to say." She leaned over to kiss his cheek.

"Pretty girl, I would never laugh at you or judge you. You are an amazing, strong, confident woman. Whatever you need to do or say is fine by me, as long as you let me stand beside you."

Zoey grabbed the flowers she'd purchased on the way.

She paused at the gate. Her gaze traveled over the cemetery. Zach watched her as she took a deep breath before reaching over to take his hand.

"There it is. It looks to be the newest one." She nodded her head toward a brown mound of dirt. No grass had grown over it yet, just sporadic weeds.

When they reached the plot, Zoey stopped short.

"Zach, this is the saddest thing I've ever seen." Tears choked in her throat. "If this was a member of our family, it would be seeded with grass already, and overflowing with flowers and tokens of our love."

Turning a tear-stained face toward him, she continued, "He lived alone. From the little I know of mental illness, he had to be completely overwhelmed trying to sort out the loneliness he lived in, and the contradicting voices in his head. And from the looks of this gravesite, he had no one to love him. Did anyone even come to see him buried? Or did some cemetery worker just drop his casket into the deep, dark ground?"

Her voice edged louder, more agitated. When he tried to

put his arms around her, she shrugged away from him. Walking to the small, non-descript headstone, she brushed the dirt from its base. Tracing fingers over the *Durgess* engraved on the stone, a small sob escaped her again.

Walking close, Zach knelt down next to her.

"Zoey Belle, he tried to hurt you. He wanted to hurt me. Don't feel bad for him." He was having a hard time wrapping his head around her reaction to seeing her attacker's grave.

"I know, Zach." Shaking her head sadly, she stood up. "I think that's why I'm having such a hard time here today. When I saw the way he lived, and now I see his sad, solitary resting place, my mind and emotions are a jumbled mess. I can't turn them off, they keep ramming into each other in my head and heart like bumper cars at the fair." She paced in front of the gravesite, rubbing her temples.

"Zoey, let's head home." He reached for her, meaning to move toward the truck.

"No, Zach. I need a moment. Don't go too far, just give me a little space. Please." She leaned in to kiss him, lips warming as they met. "Thank you. I love you so much."

He walked away, settling himself on a visitor's bench a few yards away.

Not wanting to pry into her private matters, but unable to stop himself, he strained his ears to pick up what she was saying.

"Hi, Vincent. I guess I should call you Mr. Durgess. This is so utterly ridiculous, but I can't stop myself. You attacked me, hurt me, meant to hurt the one man I've loved my entire life. Yet, I find myself hurting for you. How can I hurt for you when you hurt me? Insane, right?" She huffed out a small laugh. "Maybe I'd feel differently if you were still a threat to Zach or myself. Who knows? I'm angry with you because you wanted to hurt Zach, which would have killed me. If you were so in love with me, so in-tune with me, didn't you know that taking Zach away from me would have been as good as murdering me as well?" She stopped suddenly, glancing around at the cemetery. "But, I look around here, and it makes me sad. Where is your family? Where were your friends? What happened over the years to have you living by yourself, with no medical attention to keep your illness in check? You appeared to be very much alone in your life, and now you're very much alone in your death, and that makes me so very sad. It makes me wonder what your life could have been like if someone had loved you, taken care of you, made sure you had what you needed. Instead, I imagine you were tossed aside. Maybe not as a child, I don't know the details, but as an adult when bits and pieces of your illness made their way to the surface, did your family and friends start distancing themselves? Is that what I would have done if you'd been my friend or family?" Pausing again, Zoey took a deep, shuddering breath. "Hell, I don't know what I would have done. So here I am, mad at you for your plans and for scaring me and making me live through these last shitty months. Mad that you planned to hurt Zach. Pissed off that

I'm having to do therapy because of you. Even more pissed that I'm actually considering medication to help me sleep because of the nightmares *you* caused. Yet, my heart is hurting for you too. What if...I think it's the *what if* that's making me crazy. What if you'd went after Zach while I was in California? What if you'd knocked me down those stairs and killed me. What if someone had watched over you and helped you get the medication and attention you obviously needed?" Clearly agitated, Zoey ran her small fingers roughly through her long reddish-blonde hair.

Stopping, Zoey slowly ran a hand along the top of the headstone. Closing her eyes she whispered what Zach could only assume was a prayer because it was too quiet for him to hear.

"I'm ready to go." She gently laid the flowers she'd brought at the foot of the grave. "Goodbye, Vincent, I hope wherever you are that you're not lonely, and you're not fighting your demons any longer."

Gripping his hand, Zoey let Zach lead her to the truck. The two didn't speak until they reached his house.

"Zoey, that was..." Zach started.

"I know, it was insane. I just stood and talked to a grave. Not only that, I sympathized with my attacker, the man who planned to murder you. But, you know what, Zach? I'd do it again in a heartbeat. I want a nap before dinner at Jack and Judy's, but tonight I want to talk to the whole family. Today has opened my eyes to a lot, and I'm 100% committed to moving beyond this."

She smiled wearily, and led the way to his room. Collapsing on the bed, she murmured, "Cuddle with me while I sleep, and maybe you'll get a surprise when you wake up."

Zach shook his head, which was still spinning with thoughts of what had gone down today. She'd reacted in some ways just the way he'd thought she would. But, leave it to his Zoey Belle to find it in her heart to feel compassion for the man who introduced her to the darkness of anxiety and depression.

19

*H*e woke consumed with heat. She had obviously slept as long as she wanted to sleep, and now she wanted to play.

"Whatcha doin', pretty girl?" He held back the urge to thrust into her mouth.

Trailing kisses up his torso until she reached his chin, she smiled, "Seems like today was a good milestone for me. It's like a weight has been lifted. I remember my dad talking about feeling like he was drowning under a dark, wet blanket of blackness, and that's how I'd been feeling. But something clicked today. I'll tell you more when I talk to the whole family, but I'm feeling a little feisty right now. By my calculations, we have two hours before we need to be presentable at family dinner." Leaning it to kiss him deeply, she whispered, "You up for the challenge?"

She giggled as he thrust his length against her belly.

"I'm pretty sure I'm *up* for the challenge after being woken from my nap with your hot little mouth."

Several heavy kisses later, Zach pulled open the bedside drawer to search for the vibrator.

Stilling his search, she shook her head. "Not today, just you. I like to play sometimes, but today is a special day. I want it to be just you."

Biting back a moan in a sorry attempt to cover up what they were doing in case one of the other guys was home, Zoey panted as her body adjusted to him.

When he began to move, tears streamed from her eyes.

"Shhh, baby, what's wrong. Are you okay? Should I stop?" Zach stilled above her, his arms shaking with the effort of holding himself up.

"No, Zach, you're perfect. This is perfect." Drawing his head down to kiss her, she sighed. "Ever since the attack, there's been a piece of me that wondered if I'd ever be the same. But today was the breaking point. And having you make love to me, it cements in my heart and mind that all is going to be okay."

They shattered together, slowly floating back to earth. A playfully long, hot, distracting shower later, and they were ready to head over to Jack and Judy's for dinner.

"OH MY GOSH, it smells like she made my favorite. This day just keeps getting better and better." Zoey grinned up at Zach as he balanced the pan of crispy rice treats on his other hand.

"I'm glad we made two batches of those. They'll be gone tonight, and the pan at home won't last long before demolition. Maybe we should have hidden a couple for ourselves." Zoey laughed.

"We can make more. I know how much you like watching me in the kitchen." He winked at her.

"Mmm, you *are* pretty sexy in that apron." She couldn't hold back the laughter.

Pulling her close and nipping at her ear, Zach growled, "Don't laugh. You're the one who dared me to wear *only* the apron."

"And oh how I wish I'd been able to sneak a photo of that domestically sexy little display."

Pink cheeks, glowing smiles, they traipsed into the kitchen to find the rest of the family.

"Is that chicken and rice soup, Judy?" Zoey lifted the lid to sniff the soup.

"Yes, dear. I know you like it, and you've been having a rough time of it, so I made it for soup night. Janie is bringing chili, and Cindy volunteered vegetable beef soup. It just seemed like a soup type night." Judy patted her cheek and leaned in to kiss both of them.

"Sounds good to me." Zach winked at the older woman.

"You *have* to give me the recipe for this soup. That way I can make it for Zach sometimes."

"I'll write down what I do; there's no step-by-step recipe, but this soup is easy." Judy grabbed a notebook to write the information down for Zoey.

While the rest of the family arrived and the soups heated up, crusty loaves of bread were set to bake. Hallmark and Campbell's had nothing on Torey Hope.

Except for one thing.

"Has anyone talked to Kendrick?" Sawyer asked.

With a family as big as theirs, it was usual for several extra chairs to have been brought in, and for every nook and cranny of a room to be filled with people.

The whole room stilled when Sawyer spoke. Jeremiah cleared his throat, and all eyes traveled to him.

"I've been in contact with him. I know where he's at, but I've promised I won't let it spill for now. But I told him I wasn't going to keep quiet forever. He knows just as well as you all do that he'd be the one leading the charge if someone else had done what he did, so he doesn't get to hide away from his family. I told him if he didn't call me soon saying he was ready to come home, I was bringing you all to him. Just know he misses you all." Jeremiah smiled half-heartedly.

Dinner was a fun, boisterous, delicious affair, even if everyone missed Kendrick. When the dishes were cleared, the entire family trooped outside to sit around the fire pit.

Wine, beer, hot tea, and soda were claimed. A comfortable casualness settled over the backyard.

Zoey stood. Rubbing her hands on her pants, she looked at Zach and smiled. He nodded at her, silently encouraging whatever she had on her mind to say.

"So, I feel like I owe you all an apology and an explanation." She started, only to be cut off by The Captain.

"Zoey Belle, you don't owe us a damn thing."

"Thanks Captain, but let me finish. I feel like I owe an apology and an explanation, but I also know that the best thing I can do for all of you is to get *me* back to being *me*." She took a drink of her hot tea. Having everyone's attention, she sat back down next to Zach.

"You all know that Vincent Durgess attacked me. You've heard the police information about his infatuation with me, his mental illness, and his plans to harm Zach. Today I went to see his house. And I went to visit his grave."

When murmurs traveled through the group, Zoey paused for more tea to let the family absorb that information.

"I'm mad at Vincent, but I also hurt for him. He was a very lonely, very sick man. He didn't have the love and support that we have in this family. He had no chance against his illness, because he had no one to love him and help him. I'm relieved he's gone so we don't have to worry about him harming us, but I'm sad that he was so alone. I've felt what it's like to live under that blanket of darkness, and I know a lot of you have as well. I can't even imagine what life would be like to live with that blackness day in and day out, with no end, no help, no loving arms to wrap you in a hug."

Tears were flowing freely, but Zoey continued.

"I will get through this, and today proved that to me. I have too much to live for. I don't want to be in that forever blackness like Vincent was. I'll go to therapy, I'll even ask for the medication if it will help me relax and free me from the nightmares. But I won't shrug off the love and support that I have available to me in this family. People like Vincent Durgess don't have the privilege, but I won't waste it. I'll heal and recover. For Vincent and every other person who may have had a fighting chance if only they'd had the family I have." Reaching for Zach's hand, she went on. "When this first happened, I feared it would change me. But today I realized it's okay if it changes me, as long as I let it change me for the better. This dark period has made me more open to recognizing the greatness I have in my life. So, yes, I may change, but it's okay. Change isn't always bad. Changing is growing and growing is natural. I just don't ever want to grow away from those I love." Taking a deep breath, Zoey smiled at her family, "So, thank you all for being you. I don't want to think what it would be like trying to survive this without you all by my side. I love you."

Tearful, happy, warm hugs were given all around. When the night wound down, Zoey told Zach she wanted to go to her house for the night.

"I want to talk to you, since I seem to be in a talkative

mood today. But I want to do it in my room." Leaning in, she kissed him deeply.

"Get a room, yuck." Asher's disgusted voice startled them as he brushed by.

"Yeah, let's get a room. *My* room." Zoey winked. "But, I think Mom and Dad wanted us to go somewhere with them first."

KYLE AND JOSIE had made a phone call earlier in the day to make sure he'd be home. Driving up the expansive driveway to Jason's home, Zach just shook his head.

"I guess growing up with money and privilege could probably make most anyone a douche bag." He had never liked the guy, but he had to admit he was eternally grateful that Jason had been in San Diego to save Zoey from Vincent.

Walking to the door, the two couples held hands. Zach watched Kyle and Josie as they walked in front of him and Zoey. He'd never really dwelled on it, but Zoey was almost a clone of her mom, both physically and personality-wise. He knew Josie had overcome a lot in her past, and it gave him complete faith in Zoey being able to heal from her ordeal.

Watching Kyle playfully slap Josie's butt, Zach secretly smiled. He looked forward to growing as a couple with Zoey the way her parents had over the years.

Leaning in to whisper in Zoey's ear, he joked, "I hope we're as sexy and cool as your mom and dad when we have grown children." He chuckled as she rolled her eyes.

When Jason met them at the door, Zach wasn't sure what to expect. Would the man be back to the pretentious jackass he'd been before the attack?

It was immediately evident that Jason had changed. His clothes weren't as uppity, his smiled seemed more genuine than Zach had ever seen it, and Zach didn't feel the urge to throat punch him.

"Mr. and Mrs. Martin, please come in. Zoey, Zach." Jason offered a warm welcome. "Let's go to the kitchen, I have coffee started. I apologize for my parents not being here; they are traveling in Europe for dad's work."

With steaming mugs of coffee poured, Josie dropped Kyle's hand and walked to Jason. Drawing him into a hug, she spoke sincerely, "Jason, I want to thank you from the bottom of my heart. Thank you for saving our girl, and thank you for being by her side until you could get her home to us. Please share the contact information of your father's colleague so we can thank him for the use of his plane."

Jason humbly stepped from Josie's embrace, only to have Kyle grip him in a tight hug.

"Jason, I wasn't thrilled with you when I found out Zoey was shitfaced at your party a few years ago. But, all joking aside, you've completely redeemed yourself. Thanks so much, the words are inadequate, but they are heartfelt. Please know you're welcome in our family anytime."

Zoey walked to Jason. "Part of my nightmares include what would have happened had you not come looking for me in that stairwell. I have to believe that God put you in my life as a classmate all those years ago so that we'd have the opportunity to travel to San Diego together for the symposium. He knew I'd need you." Leaning in to kiss him on the cheek, Zoey wiped her tears and whispered, "Thank you."

Jason blushed. "I'm just glad I could be there to help." He cleared his throat, battling what appeared to be his own tears. "I have to admit my own nightmares revolve around what would have happened, but also how I could have saved you from the attack altogether if I'd not invited you to that stupid sushi dinner. I was trying to show off, impress you, and you got hurt because of my asinine thought of stealing you from Zach."

Zoey started to correct him, but Zach jumped in. "Man, if you hadn't invited her to dinner, she would have been alone. Who knows what Vincent would have done? Don't dwell on the what ifs. You saved my girl, stood by her when we couldn't, and brought her home as quickly as possible. No question, you went straight from my *douche bag* list to my *stand-up guy* list in ten seconds flat." Zach reached out and shook his hand, pulling him into a hearty half hug.

After a little chit chat, the foursome walked to the door.

Before walking into the evening, Zoey turned and laid her hand against Jason's cheek.

"This new Jason is a good look on you. You don't need to impress people, just be the great guy I know you are deep down."

Jason ducked his head, but nodded in agreement before shutting the door.

SHE SAT AT HER MIRROR, sighing as Zach slowly drew the brush through her hair. He kept his touch soft, working through tangles gently, and massaging her scalp.

"Mmmm, before you put me to sleep doing that, I wanted to talk to you about something before I bring it up to Decker."

He laid the brush down and sat on the bed as she turned from the mirror to face him.

"So, I haven't completely thought this through, but I'd really like to work with Uncle Nate, since he has a degree in counseling, and get something set up at The Center+. Not professional psychiatric help, but counseling to help people like me who are recovering from a bad incident. And maybe to help those people, like Vincent, who are suffering through darkness alone. I know years ago Libby, Audrey, and your dad had set up some talk therapy sessions at The Center+, but I'd like to look into revising the program." She stood abruptly, clearly excited and thinking about this possible next step.

He stood and drew her into a soft hug, kissing her fore-head. "I think it's a fabulous idea, and I'm sure Decker will be glad to have you helping to expand so many aspects of The Center+. I bet my dad would be more than willing to help with the counseling too. Heck, if you think about it, so many of our family have dealt with some really crappy things, I'm sure most of them would be more than willing to offer some of their time to help others through rough times. Maybe just having some people to talk to would help, and set up a more official counselor as well."

They stood silently for several moments, just savoring the touch of their bodies together.

Sighing deeply as if she'd made up her mind to speak to Decker soon, Zoey moved away from him.

"Do you remember sitting here about four years ago?" She plopped down on the bed.

"Yeah, it was probably one of the hardest days of my life. Saying goodbye to you, it tore my heart out." Zach settled in beside her on the bed.

"I remember wishing sooo badly that you'd kiss me." Zoey grinned. "God, I was so young and naïve. I want to thank you for being the level-headed one during that time. It would have been a bad move on both our parts."

"As much as I loved you then, I couldn't bring myself, as a legal adult, to kiss a kid. Just didn't sit well. It's hard to explain how I knew I loved you, knew I'd spend the rest of my life with you, knew I'd one day take you in my arms and kiss the ever-loving shit out of you, but it just wasn't right at that time." Zach shook his head at the memory.

"You said some things that really stuck with me that night. You said we were writing our own stories. You'd go off and write yours, while I wrote my own, and one day our stories would meet up again. Then we could write our story together. I never once doubted that our stories would come back together. I've never doubted that our journey would be together. I've never questioned your love for me, our love for each other."

Stopping her words, Zach grasped the back of her head pulling her in for a long, slow kiss. "Don't you *ever* doubt what we have, pretty girl. Remember, you're my forever."

"I used to think our love was perfect, and it needed to remain unflawed. But, we've seen just since you guys came home that while our *love* may be perfect, real life isn't. And that's okay. I've already told you I'd rather have *real* with you than perfect. But, ever since that day four years ago when you talked about us writing our stories separately and together, I've held onto that image. I know our story will have happy parts, and sad parts; there will be good parts and bad parts. Sometimes I'll write a chapter by myself, while you work on your own chapter. But, no matter what, I know I want to spend the rest of our lives writing this story."

"I hope you wrote those words down somewhere, because I plan on us using those as part of our wedding vows someday soon." Zach cupped her cheek, smiling mischievously.

"Zach, as romantic as it would be to have you propose to me right now, I'm going to have to pull the 'this is real life' card. I'm only 18, we aren't ready to get married yet. Plus, I'll need more time to get those vows just right."

He smiled at her somewhat panicked response.

"No worries, Zoey Belle. Part of me wants to get a ring on your finger as quickly as possible, but then I remind myself that we waited 18 years to get to this point, I think I can be patient for a few more years. As long as you're by my side." He kissed her quickly. "But, I do think we should practice our first dance as a couple."

When she looked at him questioningly, he stood from the bed and cued up his phone. Reaching for her hand, he spoke seriously, "Zoey, may I have this dance?"

Pulling her effortlessly into his arms, he spoke, "I heard this song a day or two after the attack, and it almost seemed to be mocking me. I was pissed off at a song. I felt like it was saying you needed to just brush yourself off and move on, and I knew it was going to take more than that. But each time I heard the song as you healed and got better, I realized that's exactly what you were doing. It wasn't a quick jump up and brush yourself off, you were doing it on your own time. At one point, I worried that he had shattered you too much, that I'd have to learn to love the new you. I know we're going to grow and change, but I was afraid he'd taken you from me, even though you were right there with me. But, each day we pushed you a little bit further, not wanting to go too far, but knowing the old Zoey was strong enough to handle the prodding, and praying the new Zoey was too. Watching the light come back into your eyes, the shine come back to your smile, it made *my* heart start beating again as I watched yours start beating again."

He paused and leaned his forehead against hers. "We *will* face hard times. That's not an *if*, it's a *when*. Illness, financial issues, loss of loved ones, there's no way around those things. But, we've been knocked down and gotten back up this time, and I know we'll be strong enough to do it again. So, instead of being pissed at this song, now I've sort of claimed it as *our song*."

He thumbed his phone. As "Tell Your Heart to Beat Again" by Danny Gokey filled the room, he wrapped her in his arms and they swayed to the music.

When the music ended, she lifted her tear stained face to his, "That was a beautiful song, and it's definitely ours now. Thank you for your words, I know our journey won't be easy. There will be hills and valleys, twists and turns, and plenty of roadblocks. But there's no one I'd rather be on this journey with than you."

His phone began ringing, but before he answered it, he brushed a thumb across her lips. "Still my forever girl?"

"Always your forever girl."

Kissing her deeply, he distractedly thumbed the phone to accept the call.

"Hello?"

Instantly he pulled away from her. Grasping her hand, he listened to the caller.

"Got it. No problem. We'll be there."

Disconnecting the call, he looked at Zoey.

"What? What is it?"

"It's Kendrick. We need to go."

OUT TAKES

When Zach took Zoey to her school dance because her date stood her up, he contacted Kendrick and had his cousin pay the kid a visit. Here's the scene and one of the reasons we all love Kendrick.

"Hey there, I see you're playing some ball. Care if I join?" Kendrick bestowed his signature grin on the middle school boys playing basketball at the local park.

The four boys looked a little baffled why a teenage boy like Kendrick would want to play ball with them, but they readily agreed.

As the game continued, Kendrick made chit-chat.

"What's going on over at the middle school? Looked crowded." He kept his face completely blank.

"Some stupid dance." One of the boys stated, and the rest of them broke into a fit of laughter.

Fighting to keep his composure, Kendrick continued to play it cool.

"Oh yeah, why aren't you guys there? Fine young men like yourselves probably have to fight the ladies off." He drained a three-pointer and waited on the kids to hang themselves.

"Yeah, we fight the ladies off, but we had a little bet going about tonight." The kid who spoke seemed to be the leader of the group.

"A bet? Like you bet each other you wouldn't go to the dance? Sounds pretty lame if you ask me." Kendrick was beginning to understand what had happened, but he waited for the boys to say it out loud.

"Nah, man. We each asked a girl to the dance, then dumped her. We assigned points for their reactions. Skipping the dance, getting angry, going by herself, every possible reaction earned certain points. The one of us who earned the most points gets his lunch bought for him all week at school." The boys smirked and nodded their heads as if they thought their game was awesome.

Taking a couple minutes to gather his thoughts, Kendrick dribbled and shot the ball over their head a few times. Feeling ready to deliver his smack down, he held the ball and turned to face them.

"Wow, that's...cool?" Kendrick shook his head, and made sure the boys realized he thought their bet was stupid.

"So, you let a girl buy a dress, jewelry, new shoes, do her make-up, get excited about the dance, and then stand her up...

all so you have the chance of having a cafeteria lunch bought for you?" Kendrick stopped and watched as the boys' faces to see if realization was setting in. It wasn't.

"Must have a lot better lunches at the middle school these days. Five years ago they pretty much sucked. Or at least they were bad enough I wouldn't have given up the chance to hold a girl in my arms and maybe kiss her just for a couple of free lunches."

The boys just shrugged and looked like they wished he'd leave.

No such luck.

"So, what are the points for a beautiful girl getting stood up, but her very attractive, older cousin drives her to the dance and spends the evening making sure she has the time of her life?"

"Um, well, we didn't plan for that one. Probably 5 points." The leader began to shuffle his feet, and the asswipe who'd stood Zoey up was starting to look extremely pale.

"What about the points for the girl who has a cousin who hates little shit-ass punks like you and comes to the ball courts to teach you a lesson?"

When the boys realized they'd been caught, they started to back away like they planned to leave.

"Not so fast, gentlemen."

Kendrick moved behind them and stretched his long arms to gather them all close.

"I'd say I'm worth at least 10 points. Dontcha think?" He grinned evilly and winked.

"What are you going to do to us?" The one who had stood Zoey up had trouble keeping the abject fear from his voice.

"Oh, I'm not going to hurt you, although I'd really like to hurt you the same way you hurt those three girls tonight."

"It was actually six girls..."

"Dude! Shut up, don't tell him that!"

"Ah, so not only did you each stand one girl up, you stood up multiple girls who all thought they had dates to the dance? Bravo, bravo." Kendrick shook his head in disgust.

"So, here's what you're going to do, and don't think you can skip out of it. I have two cousins, an uncle, and several friends at your school, so I'll know if you try to get out of your punishment."

He sat the boys down on the bleachers and listed his requirements.

"One, you will take each girl you stood up a flower every day this coming week. Deliver it to her at her locker. If you get punched or slapped, take it like a man because you deserve it. Two, buy a lunch and give it to a kid who looks hungry or sad or alone. Three, you won't need to buy another lunch because you'll be brown-baggin-it with bologna or PBJ from home for the entire week."

Just when he thought he was done, inspiration struck.

"Oh, and you have to sit together at a lone table, and put up a sign that says, 'We can't eat with the rest of the school because we suck for what we did.' And of course you won't breathe a word of this to anyone unless you want more punishment. I'm betting your parents had no clue you made the bet and planned to hurt those girls.'"

By the time the boys scrambled from the bleachers and ran from the park, Kendrick was laughing and truly wished he'd be able to watch the lunch room this week. He'd make sure Uncle Nate knew what was going on. He knew Zoey and Aly would keep him apprised of the boys' progress in their week-long punishment.

He headed home while he texted Zach, "It's all taken care of, dude."

The past year or so had been rough on Kendrick. He reveled in being able to forget his troubles and just help his family. When he was joking around or messing with punk-ass kids, he wasn't thinking about how much the past couple years had sucked.

NOTES

Zoey received training in Neurokinetic Therapy. You can find out more about this practice here http://neurokinetictherapy.com/

Lasagna gardening articles:

http://www.motherearthnews.com/organic-gardening/lasagna-gardening-zmaz99amztak.aspx

http://organicgardening.about.com/od/startinganorganic garden/a/lasagnagarden.htm

http://www.thriftyfun.com/Lasagna-Gardening-Tips.html

http://www.urbanfarmonline.com/urban-gardening/backyard-gardening/lasagna-gardening.aspx

Books about lasagna gardening:
http://amzn.to/1JNBN4i

NOTES

I started writing my first book (For Nicky) in October 2013; I had no clue if I could do it, and even less clue about what to do when I finished it. About halfway through that book, I realized that the mean, terrible sister, Audrey, had a story to tell; I started Because of Beckett as soon as I finished For Nicky.

I had no intention of continuing the Torey Hope Series. However, readers had fallen in love with the stories and they asked for more. I created a heartwarming Christmas novella to lead into the third full-length novel, Loving Josie.

One day, in the shower (where else do great ideas come from?), I realized that the younger generation of Torey Hope had some stories to tell. I ran the idea by readers, and they loved the prospect of continuing the Torey Hope Series. So, voila, Torey Hope: *The Later Years* was born! You can read Decker and Sawyer HERE and HERE.

One of these days, I'll let the other characters and stories out of my head and create some new books and series; until then, I continue to fall in love with the hearts of my Torey Hope characters in each and every story.

THANK YOU FOR READING! I hope you enjoyed; please take a moment to leave a review. If you're reading on a file/device that doesn't take you to a review option, you may click here to leave a review on Amazon. bit.ly/ZachAmazon

A.D. Ellis

ABOUT THE AUTHOR

A.D. Ellis spends the majority of her days loving and wrangling two school-aged children, a husband, and a Yorkie with a stubborn streak a mile wide before heading to the inner city of Indiana to teach a challenging group of alternative education students in grades third through sixth. Most days she hits the gym after school in hopes of running and lifting away the stress and headaches of the day before picking up her children and squeezing a whole day's worth of loving and living into the too-short hours before bed. It's no wonder Ms. Ellis lives for the slower, easier days she gets to enjoy on breaks from school.

Growing up in a small farming town in southern Indiana, A.D. is grateful to her mother for passing along the love of reading. With her nose constantly stuck in a book, Ms. Ellis became accustomed to friends and acquaintances snickering and shaking their heads at her love of reading.

A.D. never dreamed of being anything but a teacher, although there are certain times of the year when she laments her career choice. Ms. Ellis had a story idea floating in her head for about a year. After persistent prodding from a friend, A.D. put pen to paper and began writing her first story in October 2013. From that moment on, she was hooked. Taking the people and stories from her head and sharing them with readers is a scary, exhausting, rewarding, and fulfilling experience which A.D. plans to continue until there are no more stories banging around in her mind.

A.D. Ellis' work can be found on two major platforms including Amazon. Please contact her on Facebook, Twitter, or her website.

Amazon bit.ly/AmazonADEllis

Facebook www.facebook.com/adellisauthor

Twitter www.twitter.com/ADEllisAuthor

Website www.adellisauthor.com

ACKNOWLEDGMENTS

This is always one of the hardest parts of finishing a book, but quite possibly the most important part! It's so hard because I fear I'll miss someone who has helped me out, supported me, been a listening ear, or offered advice and encouragement. If I miss listing your name here, please know it wasn't on purpose, and I love you dearly!

To my editor, Stephanne, thank you from the bottom of my heart for your sharp eyes and constant professionalism. You were a gift to me over 10 years ago, and you continue to be a blessing.

To my friend, fellow author, and cover designer, Andrea Michelle at Artistry in Design. Thank you for taking my vision and bringing it to life through your design. I love you!

To my dear beta readers. Your input, feedback, and encouragement has proven invaluable to me! I truly trust you all and value your opinions more than you'll probably ever understand.

To my street team/pimpers. Those of you who list me in contests and comments and shout outs all the time, you're amazing and I love you for always working to get my name out there! If I start naming people here, I'll be sure to miss some; just know if you've ever shared my name or my books, it means the world to me and I appreciate you more than you'll ever know!

To my READERS!! Without you, there would have never been a third book, let alone a seventh book! Thank you for loving Torey Hope and the characters as much as I do; knowing you are looking forward to another book is a lot of what keeps me writing some days. As long as these stories are in my head, I'll keep sharing them with you.

To the BLOGGERS who read and review and share my books!! You are beyond a shadow of a doubt some of the most dedicated and selfless people I've ever known! Thank you so much for being such a support to those of us who have stories to tell. I love BLOGGERS!

To my girls at The Indie Erogenous Zone. You are beyond fellow authors, you're my support, my heart, my friends. There have been days I wanted to give up, but I had you to turn to; days when a bad review breaks my heart, but I talk it out with you. I truly consider you all my close friends and I wouldn't want to be facing this crazy journey without you! IEZ4Life! T&F girls!

To my Juice Box ladies! Thank you so much for welcoming me into your crew and sharing your knowledge, experience, advice, and fun with me! Having some real-life authors/friends I can collaborate with is a great feeling. Dance parties, lunches, movies, videos, wine, painting, pizza...the list goes on and on! Thank you for letting me be a Juice Boxer!

To my fellow authors. Those of you who read my work, share your work with me, cross-promote with me, and offer advice and support, THANK YOU! You make this a little easier and enjoyable.

Thank you to Megg M. for the info you provided to me about the neurokinetic training Zoey was attending. And, Julie E, thank you for your input about some conflict in this story. I appreciate you both!

To my family and friends. I know most of you don't understand my obsession with getting these stories out of my head and on paper, but you're proud of me either way. Some of you get to read my books, some of you get to see cover ideas, some of you have to watch me lose myself in a story, some of you have to hear me vent about the hard parts of all of this; all of you love me and support me and for that, I am truly lucky and grateful.

CONNECT WITH A.D. ELLIS

Follow my Amazon author page for updates http://bit.ly/AmazonADEllis or find me on Facebook http://www.facebook.com/adellisauthor

If you want to get updates about releases, interviews, sales, giveaways, and more please sign up for my newsletter bit.ly/EllisNewsletter

You can also find me on Twitter http://www.twitter.com/ADEllisAuthor

Find me on Spotify if you'd like to listen to the playlist for this book (mainly just the songs I listened to while writing) or any of my other books. Just search for A.D. Ellis.

RECIPES

Recipes

Cucumber, Lemon, Mint Water

This is a quick and easy recipe from the author's mom.

In a pitcher of water, cut slices of cucumber and lemon. Add sprigs of mint.

Pour over glasses of ice.

Enjoy!

CRISPY RICE TREATS

3 tablespoons butter

1 package (10 oz., about 40) JET-PUFFED Marshmallows

OR

4 cups JET-PUFFED Miniature Marshmallows

6 cups crisped rice cereal

DIRECTIONS

1)   In large saucepan melt butter over low heat. Add marshmallows and stir until completely melted. Remove from heat.

2)   Add crisped rice cereal. Stir until well coated.

3)   Using buttered spatula or wax paper evenly press mixture into 13 x 9 x 2-inch pan coated with cooking spray. Cool. Cut into 2-inch squares. Best if served the same day.

MICROWAVE DIRECTIONS:

In microwave-safe bowl heat butter and marshmallows on HIGH for 3 minutes, stirring after 2 minutes. Stir until smooth. Follow steps 2 and 3 above. Microwave cooking times may vary.

CHICKEN and RICE SOUP

This is a favorite soup of the author's. As with Judy Jordan, the author's mom used no exact recipe, but she swears it's easy.

1)   Cook 13-18 chicken wings in water until tender.

2)   Take the wings out.

3)   Into the broth put a cup of finely chopped celery, half cup finely chopped onions. Cook until tender.

4)   Try to have at least 4 quarts of broth water.

5) After veggies are tender, put in one and a half cup of long cooking rice. Simmer until rice has cooked.

6) Put in the chicken you take off the wings.

7) Little paprika, salt, pepper.

Optional:

After step 6, add in heavy cream and let it simmer (this is the way the author likes it best!)

On step 3, depending on your mood, you can add in other chopped veggies in addition to the celery and onion.

EXCERPTS FROM OTHER TOREY HOPE NOVELS

EXCERPTS FROM OTHER TOREY HOPE NOVELS

These books are the beginning of the Torey Hope books. The parents and grandparents in Decker *are the main characters in these earlier books.*

A *Torey Hope Novel Series* starts with For Nicky. Meet and fall in love with Nate and Nicky Morgan, twin brothers. Find For Nicky here: http://bit.ly/NickyAmazon

"Hey, Audrey, what's up? Come in." Audrey smiles, which seems a little fake, and comes on in. She's dressed to the nines as usual. Heels, tight skirt, tighter shirt, hair styled much bigger than you'd think is possible. I can smell her perfume and hairspray as she walks past me. Who dresses like this for a normal day? Audrey does, obviously. She looks me up and down. "Are you going somewhere, Beth?"

I tell her I have a date. She looks pissed for a moment, then gives me a smile that doesn't even begin to reach her eyes, and says, "Oh, that's nice. Who's the poor shmuck?"

Obviously, she's baiting me, but I don't think quickly enough and I just reply, "Nathaniel Morgan."

*Audrey rolls her eyes. "Beth, sweetie, I'm going to try to say this in the nicest/sisterly love type of way. But, Nathan Morgan is way out of your league. You are dressed in a flannel shirt, you might as well wear a sign that says 'frumpy' on the front and 'won't ever get laid' on the back. Nate is an animal in bed, I should know. He needs sex. I doubt you're giving it to him yet. If you ever decide to try sex again, it will probably be as bad as it was with Austin. Not because Nate isn't good, because the good Lord knows that man is G.O.O.D in bed, but there's no way your 'basically a virgin' body can live up to what he's used to. Hell, the boy wore ME out and I have as much experience as he does, if not more. I'm not sure why he's hung around this long. Maybe he sees you as a challenge. Yeah, maybe he's decided to string you along long enough to get in your pants, but, Beth, he's not going to stick around. Nate needs hot sex, a variety of girls, no strings. I don't want you to get hurt when he fucks you and leaves you. Oh, God, Beth, seriously, stop with the teary puppy-dog eyes. I'm just telling you the truth." ∼Libby {Beth} Decker in **For Nicky**__*

∼

THE SEQUEL TO FOR NICKY, Because of Beckett (this is Audrey's story and as much as you hate her in For Nicky, you will find yourself liking her in Because of Beckett and you will fall in love with Jeremiah Jordan!) Find Because of Beckett here: http://bit.ly/BeckettAmazon

The one girl he should stay as far away from as possible, the one girl who had made him feel more alive in one evening than he had in several years, the one girl who threatened his well-designed single-dad, good role model position in life was Audrey Decker. Instead of letting her off the hook and planning the party himself, he had practically begged her to stick with it and all but promised her there would be no problems. That was all well and good, he was truly glad she was going to take the party, except for one small problem, he hadn't been able to get her out of his mind; he couldn't stop thinking of those gorgeous blue eyes or her beautiful hair or luscious curves. His heart jumped into his throat when he saw her walking toward the shelter house; his breath hitched in his chest when her hand touched his knee; he wanted to hold her hand and start right back where they had left off the other night. But, they'd agreed that this was a business deal only, so he wouldn't complicate it. They'd get through the party and move on. They were living in the same town; they'd surely see each other. Jeremiah was determined to keep things cool between them so the party would be a success and they could be friendly toward each other in social settings.

And then, he watched her eyes light up as she knelt down

*and opened her arms to Beckett. He was gone; hook, line, sinker. Audrey didn't strike him as the type to be particularly caring towards anyone, let alone a child with special needs. But, there she was, on her knees, hugging his son... How was it, the woman he had just promised he wouldn't pursue, was on the ground hugging his child like his real mother never had? Jeremiah's gut clenched at the thought. He wanted this woman in his life. But, she'd made it clear that she wasn't interested and Jeremiah wondered if he had lost his chance to indicate any interest. So, he decided he'd have to settle for having her in his life as a friend. ~Jeremiah Jordan in **Because of Beckett**

THE FAMILIES CELEBRATE the holidays in Christmas in Torey Hope, A Novella. Love and family and friendship abounds and readers get to learn of the older couples' love stories. Find Christmas in Torey Hope here: http://bit.ly/ChristmasAmazon*

"Libby-girl, you never cease to amaze me. That was amazing." He kissed her and they proceeded to clean up and redress. "Now, we better get back to the house before everyone knows what I've been doing to you." Nate winked.

Libby's cheeks blushed but she said, "Nate, I'm pretty sure this is exactly what your mom had in mind when she sent us away for a bit."

"Well then, I'll have to sincerely thank my momma!" Nate kissed her lips as they headed back out the door, locking it soundly behind them.

"Uh, Mom, I'm all for reminiscing and I know you and Dad love each other, but could we please keep it G-rated. For the love of all that is good, please don't make me listen to sex stories involving you two." Jeremiah shuddered but smiled good-naturedly at his mother.

"What? We all had to see you and Audrey and Nate and Libby come in here glowing after your little 45 minute romp; I think a little steamy romance story about your dad and I would serve you right." Judy laughed at her son's expression. "Don't worry, I'll keep it clean." The whole group laughed at Jeremiah's visible relief.

Before the story *could get started, Nate cleared his throat and said, "Mom, Dad, let's keep in mind that I've walked in on the two of you in some compromising positions that are now burned into my delicate mind; please don't add anymore trauma to my already*

scarred psyche." Everyone laughed at Nate's statement. "You all think I'm joking but I'm really not. You don't know the images that still float through my mind." Nate teased his parents and pulled Libby against him as they settled onto one of the couches.

L<small>OVING</small> J<small>OSIE</small> IS a story of second chance love for two lost souls. This is a standalone novel in A Torey Hope Novel Series, so you can read it without reading the first books. Find Loving Josie here: http://bit.ly/LovingJosieAmazon

"What the hell are you thinking, Josie Decker?" This from Audrey. She continued, "I just left my house after calling in my reinforcements here. Did you know Kyle's over at my house talking to Jeremiah? He's all dressed up, pierced up, tatted up, bleached up, and styled up. Do you know why? He's got a date. Oh, but that's right, you already knew he had a date, didn't you?!"

When I didn't respond, because I wasn't sure if this was a rhetorical question or not, she powered on. "It was bad enough when you bought a house with the man. But now you're going to 'pretend date' him?! This isn't a good thing, Josie. If he weren't so fucked up, I would be cheering you on. And, honestly, I think dating you would be truly good for him. But, he's so damn stubborn, I worry he'll never let go of the notion that he can't love you the way you deserve and, in the end, you're going to end up being hurt." ~Josie Decker in ***Loving Josie***

TURNING *me around he tipped my chin up, "We need to talk, Jo. Some things have changed. No more practice dating. No more stopping kisses and pretending they shouldn't happen. I want to see more than my ink on you; I want to see me on you." With that final comment he brought his mouth down on mine. This kiss was different than all of the others had been. This kiss was all Kyle, he was holding nothing back.* ~Josie Decker in ***Loving Josie***

DECKER, *Torey Hope: The Later Years* (this is the first book in the new series) bit.ly/DeckerAmazon

"Hello, this is Decker Morgan at The Center+. I'm calling for Ms. Katherine Turner in regards to her recent resume and job application." Decker held the phone away from his ear as he heard an earsplitting blare coming through the line.

"Oh my God! I'm so sorry! Hold on please, Mr. Morgan!

This is Katherine Turner....hang on just a second! Where's the damn broom?!" A cacophony came through the phone and Decker was tempted to hang up; if this was the way Ms. Turner conducted herself on the phone she was obviously not the one for the job.

"Shut up, damn it! Just shut up!" Her words were barely distinguishable over the shrill alarm-like noise. "There! I'm so sorry, Mr. Morgan. Mr. Morgan? Sir? Are you there? Please accept my apologies. I was helping my grandma bake cookies. I didn't realize that Grandma had accidentally turned the oven up to 500 and the timer to thirty-one minutes rather than thirteen minutes. Needless to say, our little cookies are now burnt offerings. On the bright side, we know her smoke detectors work." Katherine Turner spoke in an airy, breathless way that had Decker picturing her in a smoky kitchen, hair askew, with a broomstick to turn off the offending smoke detector.

"Well, Ms. Turner, you're the first applicant I've called who has provided so much entertainment in such a short amount of time. I trust that there's no danger to you or your grandmother?" Decker really couldn't explain why he felt the need to continue with this phone interview; the girl obviously wasn't management material, but he wanted to hear her answers to his questions because she had him feeling something he hadn't felt in a long time. Intrigued.

Forty-five minutes later, Decker hung up from the most enjoyable phone interview he'd ever conducted. Katherine Turner was not the typical uptight management applicant that he'd been speaking to; this woman was genuine, whip-smart, well-spoken, and on the same path as him. It amazed him just how much they had in common both personally and professionally. Before ending the call with her, Decker had done something he'd never planned on doing; he offered her the job over the phone, sight unseen, no further interview. She had accepted, and he was pumped to meet her in person the next day and get the paperwork filled out so she could get to work right away.

Looking at the clock, he realized that it was late enough he could call it a day. There was really nothing else he needed to do right then. He texted his brother to see if Sawyer wanted to play some basketball before they headed home. As it turned out, Sawyer's meeting with the potential martial arts instructor had run over so he wasn't available; Zach, Kendrick, and Decker played a little game before their dads and uncle showed up. Nate Morgan, Jeremiah Jordan, and Kyle Martin had been playing ball together for years and gave the younger men a run for their money. In the end, all six men were sweaty but laughing. Decker paused as he left The Center+ on his way home. Yeah, it was good to be back.

"UNKNOWN CALLER" flashed on his phone screen as he worked on some paperwork for Katherine Turner. Absent-mindedly he picked up the phone, "Decker Morgan."

"Hello, Mr. Morgan. I'm really sorry to call you at home in the evening, but you gave me your number and said I could call if I had any questions. I have to apologize, I think the whole cookie burning had me flustered today; I don't normally accept a job sight-unseen and without meeting my boss in person. I still plan on coming in tomorrow, but I was hoping to discuss the position with you a little more now that the smoke has cleared from both my head and my grandma's kitchen. That is, if you have a moment to speak to me." He admired her straightforwardness and knew she was just as knocked off-kilter as he was after their whirlwind phone interview earlier that day.

"I have time, Ms. Turner. Please, ask anything you'd like." Decker waved to Sawyer as his brother popped his head in the office to say hello. Plopping down on the couch, Decker stretched his 6'2" frame out and got comfortable.

"Well, I've been doing some research on The Center+, but I'd like to hear your description of it. Please." Katherine had a smile in her voice as she added the please to her request.

"The Center+ has been a part of my family's life since long before I was born. My Uncle Nicky attended school there and my Grandma Cindy worked there as an administrative assistant for several years. Uncle Nicky had finished schooling, but he attended several recreational programs even after high school and he met the new librarian, Libby Decker who later married my dad. Not long after, my Uncle Nicky met my Aunt Carly while they were both working there. When my brother and cousins and I were younger, we spent almost every spare second at The Center+, although it was just The Center in those days. We enjoyed all of the programs available and took full advantage of the recreational sports. We used to always talk about growing up, going to college, and coming back to Torey Hope to expand the programs; make The Center+ bigger and better than ever. That brings us to today; we are adding two new wings, several new programs, revamping and improving the sports program, and enlarging the arts program by leaps and bounds. My family owns The Center+ now, so we have the ability to grow the business as we've always dreamed." Decker paused in his description; on the other end of the phone Katherine was touched at the sense of pride the man had in his family's business.

Several minutes later, Katherine had asked as many questions as she could come up with and their conversation turned to more personal information. Decker learned that she had also recently graduated and returned to Torey Hope, her childhood home. She and her mother lived across town and her elderly grandmother lived with them. She had always planned to leave Torey Hope for college and thought she would move to the big city, but when her mom divorced and her grandmother moved in she took inventory of her life and her plans for her future and realized that Torey Hope was her heart, and she didn't want to leave.

Decker found himself lulled by the melodic lilt of her voice and nodded in agreement with her that finding a business management job in a small town was a definite challenge. He smiled when she shared her excitement over the potentially perfect job opportunity he had presented her with.

Through their conversation, Decker felt a definite connection to this girl; she shared his vision for success, she was a hard worker, she was self-motivated, she was a people person, she knew how to get a job done. She was perfect. Damn, the first girl he'd ever felt truly drawn to was going to be his assistant manager which meant that the connection he felt to her couldn't go anywhere. One of his hard and fast rules was that business and pleasure never mixed. Never.

"Well, Mr. Morgan, thanks for answering my questions. I feel a little bit more at ease over my spur-of-the-moment acceptance of this job. I just want to say one thing, please remember how perfect I am for the job when you meet me again tomorrow." Katherine had a smile in her voice as she spoke. "Goodnight, Mr. Morgan."

Meet her again? What the hell did that mean?

Sawyer, Torey Hope: *The Later Years* (bit.ly/SawyerAmazon1)

Sawyer, age 16

Shirts discarded and arms entangled around torsos, the young men rolled around the bed as if wrestling. Hidden, she watched from the doorway in fascination, not disgust or horror. Her mind struggled to make sense of something her heart had already accepted. As the boys' lips met in a sensual kiss, she brought her hand up to cover her surprise. She knew, instinctively, the act happening in front of her was what Sawyer had been missing, seeking, craving.

Knowing she should look away, afford them privacy, she couldn't unglue her eyes from the awkwardly arousing scene transpiring before her. Hands roamed, cupping ass cheeks; hips and tongues thrust in simultaneous dances. Red basket-ball shorts and tight gray boxer briefs slid down firm, muscular legs followed quickly by black shorts and black briefs moving down a second pair of toned legs. She'd seen the male anatomy in Health class, but the young men on the bed were aroused from their sensuous exploration and she felt her eyes widening in impressed awe at the size of their... male anatomy. Sawyer, the dark haired one, reached a hand down and grasped the other boy; the act was reciprocated and a delightful display began to play out before her. Mouths, teeth, and tongues clashed as hips thrust and fists pumped; rough breaths, sexually charged, resonated in the otherwise silent room.

She knew she should have left, should have allowed him this intimate moment, but it was too late; an ill-timed sneeze, obstructed by a quick pinch to the nose, but not thwarted completely, literally blew her cover.

Walking arm-in-arm, they headed back toward his house. "So, Josh, huh? Do you want him to be, like, your boyfriend?" Katie nudged Sawyer's hip in teasingly playful way.

"I like Josh, but I think I like him because he's the first guy I've kissed. I like his body next to mine; I like to have my hands on him; I like to kiss him. Do I like *him*? I don't know. I don't think he's any closer to admitting or accepting his sexuality than I am, so I don't see us becoming a couple and publicly outing ourselves. If anything, we'll spend time behind *closed* doors and try to figure things out for ourselves, individually." Katie blushed at the mention of *closed* doors.

"Hey, bud, that door was practically wide open. I probably should have just walked away, but you two were astonishingly beautiful in your sexy little coupling, and I couldn't help myself. You should thank your lucky stars it was me and not your mom or dad or brother!" Katie wagged a finger sternly in front of his face.

Sawyer blanched yet again at the thought of his parents or twin brother, Decker, finding him in a compromising position with another man. He knew in his heart that his parents and brother would accept him no matter what, but he didn't want to bring undue stress or drama into their lives; for now, he'd keep it secret, but he'd tell them once he was a little more comfortable with it himself.

But, the thing with keeping secrets and not being truthful with those who love you is that it gets harder and harder with each day. As the years passed, Sawyer realized he'd missed several prime opportunities to be upfront with his parents and Decker.

I'm gay.

His brother, Decker, had taken the news fairly well. He'd needed a solo walk through the woods to gather his thoughts; Sawyer suspected his always-in-control, serious, black and white brother also needed to come to grips with the fact that he'd never suspected his brother's sexual preference was different than his own. How ironic that the one person Sawyer was the closest to in the whole world was the one person who was the most clueless.

Sawyer had held his breath practically the whole time Decker had been walking through the woods. A deluge of rain poured down as the dark sky broke open, yet Sawyer still sat alone at the campfire. His head had started playing tricks on him. *You disgust him...he can't stand the thought of having a gay brother...you've lost him...he's not coming back.* But Sawyer held out hope that Decker was just doing his usual thinking things through.

He had breathed a sigh of relief when Decker emerged,

soaking wet, from the woods. Walking towards him with purpose, his twin had stopped in front of him and spoke the most heartwarming, sincere words Sawyer had ever heard from him.

"You're my brother, always have been, always will be. I wish you could have told me sooner, but nothing has changed between us. I'll be there in any and every way that I can." Decker grabbed Sawyer and pulled him into a deep embrace, communicating his love and acceptance through his touch.

Telling his cousins, Zach and Kendrick, had been less emotional, and a lot more entertaining. Sawyer had to laugh at the questions his admission had stirred up.

"I'm gay."

Two words that held such power. Would they laugh? Would they walk away in disgust? Would they be angry?

Zach smiled and nodded. "I think I've known that for a long time, man, but thanks for telling me."

"Wait, you knew? Why didn't you ever say something? Why did you joke with me about girls?"

"I don't know, I guess I figured you'd tell me when you were ready. I didn't want to bring it up if I was wrong and it offended you. I think I joked about girls thinking it would give you the opportunity to bring it up if you wanted to." Zach stood and walked to his cousin, reaching a hand down, he pulled the other man up into a hug. *"Nothing changes, I've got your back, man."*

Kendrick sat with his hand rubbing his chin. Would he be the one who couldn't accept it?

Eyes twinkling and a shit-eatin' grin on his face, he finally spoke. "What's it like to suck cock?"

If you'd like to read any or all of the books from which I've shared excerpts, please find them on my Amazon Author Central page HERE.

www.ingramcontent.com/pod-product-compliance
Lightning Source LLC
Chambersburg PA
CBHW021209250626
47155CB00008B/2745